THE SERVANT

# The Servant

ALISTAIR McALPINE

faber and faber

First published in 1992
by Faber and Faber Limited
3 Queen Square London WC1N 3AU

Phototypeset by Intype, London
Printed in England by
Clays Ltd, St Ives plc

A CIP record for this book is available from the British Library

ISBN 0–571–16886–8

2 4 6 8 10 9 7 5 3 1

To the most magnificent, Baroness Thatcher of Kesteven,
Prime Minister of Great Britain 1979–1990,
from one of her many servants,
who believes she could have been better served.

When he wrote *The Prince*, Machiavelli was presenting himself for a job. Of all the activities of idle men, politics can be the most exciting, and those like Machiavelli left stranded by its tides will always try to return. Machiavelli believed that through his knowledge of history he could show a Prince how to conduct himself, how to apply techniques learned from historical events to his advantage. But history is a fallible guide, and it is curious that a man seeking employment from a successful Prince should presume to advise him on his conduct. Instead of instructing the Prince, a more Machiavellian Machiavelli would have written a book advising the Servants of Princes. The Prince, identifying a talent for service, would have hired him on the spot, granting Machiavelli the influence he so desired. That book, which might also have been called *The Servant*, would have explained not how Machiavelli could assist the Prince in governing his country, but how he would serve him by dealing on his behalf as the Prince acted in matters great and small: clearing a path for the Prince to rule, managing day by day those around him. Such a book would recognize that while politicians have the same frailties and failings, fears and conceits as all other human beings, they live in a closeted environment which heightens their senses and makes them act irrationally. It is because politicians are human yet may not behave like other humans that the Servant cannot be totally straightforward. On occasions the Servant needs to deceive and mislead – not for pleasure or gain, but to ensure the success of the Idea and the Prince. This book tries to show some of the devices that can be used to ensure the advancement of the Idea through securing the rule of the Prince.

The Idea is unique to the Prince. The Idea is the philosophy on which the Prince will base all of his actions. The Idea incorporates the Prince's aims and ambitions for his people. The Idea explains how the Prince's kingdom will grow and how it will compete with the kingdoms of other leaders. The Idea will become the touchstone for the morals of his people. The Idea starts with the Prince, and while men and women may say that they advise the Prince, they will really be attracted by the power of the Idea. It is from the Idea that the Prince draws his strength. The Prince needs the Idea in order to be able to take the necessary decisions to gain power in the land and then hold on to that power. Without the Idea this man is nothing.

In this book when I speak of the Prince I do not mean just any leader. I speak of the perfect Prince, with all the nobility of spirit that the greatest of Princes should have. The Prince governs for the benefit of the people. The Prince governs only for this reason. It is to promote the Idea that the Prince rules. He is not a Prince who merely by chance finds himself in charge of the affairs of other men. If the Prince finds that after a time other men have frustrated his intention of carrying out his Idea and so decides to change his Idea, then he must cease to be the Prince. In just holding a job his conduct is such that he is not truly the Prince, not a leader for the Servant to serve and not a man to be trusted with the Idea. It has been said that there is nothing so powerful as an idea when its time is come. The Servant's role is to serve the Prince in the implementation of the Idea, to do what he can to ensure the time *is* the right one.

The Servant is the instrument of the Prince and the Idea, not of the state. The state has its own servants, who owe it their loyalty, because Princes and Ideas inevitably change.

In these pages, when I speak of the Servant I mean perhaps one man, or possibly the leader's private office. I do not speak of the whole of the Prince's court, or the cabinet of a political leader, although the collective Servant can contain members of a court or a cabinet. I will in this work speak of the concept of service on its highest possible plane. The difference between the Prince and the Servant is that the Prince as a ruler has power: the Servant could use power, power that comes from his relationship with the Prince, but chooses to use influence instead. It is the Servant's job to help explain the Idea to its followers, to enlist and to organize their support. The Servant will use the Idea to inspire the wealthy supporters of the Prince and collect from them large sums. The Servant will also use the Idea to raise small sums from the multitude of people, for if a man supports an idea with his money, no matter how small the sum, then that support can generally be relied upon at moments when the Prince's right to rule is tested. This money that the Servant raises will be used to run the Prince's campaign, to purchase the advice of experts in the arts of influencing the opinion of the people. The Prince's essential task is to formulate and preach the Idea, but although the Servant will organize his campaigns, it is vital that the direction of these campaigns lies exclusively in the hands of the Prince. It is of the utmost importance that the Prince knows that it is he who won the throne, and he alone. Afterwards many will claim the glory for these victories, of course. But the Prince who was indeed placed in power by other men's efforts appreciates that he can also be removed by their efforts, will live always with this thought and will rule with uncertainty. The Prince who wins by his own efforts will feel secure, although when men tell of the battles fought to win that power he will not wish to hear others take any credit that he himself has not bestowed.

People will find it hard to trust a Prince who comes to power through fortune or who is implicated with those who have stolen power. He must always beware, for in moments when he is weak the people will remember this of him. A Prince can rule only with an Idea — can only rule with lasting success, that is — and having stolen power without an Idea he can merely play the part of a Prince, waiting for others to pull him down. The Servant must orchestrate the Prince's campaigns, for he understands the working of organizations. The Prince may by chance understand organizations, but he must concentrate on directing the thrust of his campaigns and preaching the Idea. Ideas need an organization to make their time come, but an organization is completely different from an Idea. An Idea increases in strength by staying the same, while an organization increases in strength by changing opportunistically. Experience is of great advantage to an organization, of no advantage to an Idea. Only if the Idea is not adulterated will it come to dominance.

The Servant will understand the grandeur of his role, for in the heart of every Servant there lies a Prince — a desire to be noble and brave and successful. It is proper that this should be so, for the Prince is a symbol of all these things. But, Servant, let that inner Prince lie still, for ambition is easily spotted and becomes the wasting disease of the able Servant. Contain this force, this ambition, and use its energy only in the service of your master, and in time you may become a Prince among Servants.

[4]

To carry out his work the Servant will need a myth – by which I mean the sum of a variety of personae which the Servant assumes. The myth is how the Servant disguises himself while moving among his contemporaries, it is the facade behind which the Servant hides from those who would know him well. This is not the careful rearrangement of his character for the benefit of future historians, but a device that the Servant uses in his daily contact with people who see him often and know him well. Indispensable to the Servant, the myth must be chosen with care, but not because this is how the Servant would like to appear to his fellow men – the true Servant would never engage in such conceit. The Servant's myth is chosen solely for its ability to help the Servant to serve the Idea and the Prince. The myth of the Servant has three main strands: love, fear and hate. Loyalty plays no part in the world inhabited by Princes and their Servants, and to believe in it leads only to betrayal and deep disappointment. Loyalty is the stuff of romantic novelists, the attribute of faithful dogs and horses. In the circle of the Prince and the Servant loyalties change with circumstances. If by chance you find loyalty be grateful, but never expect loyalty or assume it in your plans. Is the Servant loyal? He is loyal to the Prince and the Idea, but only to both because he believes in both, and only while both are joined together. Belief is a much stronger instinct than loyalty: loyalty is the emotion which remains after belief has died.

Machiavelli says that the Prince should endeavour 'to escape being hated', but hatred forms a strand in the Servant's myth. Although it must be perfumed and powdered and heavily disguised, a little hatred in a myth hones it like a sharpening stone. It gives the myth force, but, most importantly, it is the flaw which will give it credibility. Fear is another ingredient. It is always useful to be a little feared, though the fear must be inspired by the position held rather than the man himself.

[5]

On the other hand, love should be present in abundance, since it helps disguise the less attractive aspects of strength. Love suggests commitment, a very attractive quality; it also suggests that there is a weakness in the Servant – that he is capable of irrational thought, that for those he loves there is no point beyond which he will not go. Remember that I am talking of the Servant's myth, not the Servant in truth. While the Servant may or may not be capable of love, he allows no true love to touch his judgement. Love is a very important factor, for if the Servant will convince others of the Idea, he must first fall in love with it himself. Love is the most powerful weapon of a Servant who would change people's minds, for some, seeing how much the Servant loves the Idea, will pay attention to it, and others, seeing how the Servant loves them, will listen to him. If the Servant is to convince a man of an Idea, he must love the man. If the man is objectionable, the Servant must never say so; indeed, he must never even think that this man is objectionable – thoughts communicate quite as easily as words. Love for another is the highest form of flattery because it seems to the beloved an endorsement of their views, which is vital if you would change those views. When I use the word 'love' I use it in an emotional sense; the Servant must never be drawn into physical contact with someone whose mind he seeks to change. Lesser men than the Servant may lust after the body of another, and may excuse this lust to themselves saying, 'I love this one and seduce this one in the interests of my occupation, for it will help my career, and in the interests of the Prince, for by this physical love I can change this one's mind.' This is a trap; have none of it.

There are, of course, many other strands in the Servant's myth besides love, fear and hate, but these three provide the essential emotional foundation for his work. This myth must be believed by all but the Servant himself. He must, before he engages in myth-making, discover the nature of his true character. Only then will he be able in times of great difficulty to tell the difference between himself and his myth, between the truth and the perceived truth. The Servant moves like a shadow behind his own myth. Yet although he may cynically construct the myth, which he knows to be a device, the Idea he must truly believe in; he must allow no cynicism to creep into the Idea. As he exploits his myth, directing it to take this or that action, he must take care not to destroy it. It must be so constructed that, when he is carrying out his tasks, the Servant does not find himself in conflict with the myth. There will be occasions when events are so dire that the Servant has to take action that brings him into conflict with the myth. When creating the myth it is well to take this into account. Reasons for such conflict must be built into the myth and carefully concealed, only to be revealed in an emergency. Revealing them will explain to the population this apparent inconsistency in the Servant's character. Although the myth and the actions of the Servant are some-times totally different, and indeed can operate in different directions at the same time, the Servant must never have to choose between necessary action and his myth. This will give the Servant great strength, for people will judge him by what they know of his myth. People like to be reassured; the public respect uniform, both military and civilian, and like to believe that they know exactly what they are dealing with. The people, never truly knowing the Servant, will never truly know how he will behave.

If it becomes publicly known that the Servant and his myth are not one and the same thing, then the Servant would do well to consider early retirement and a career in agriculture. Agriculture, or gardening which is its most civilized form, is a wonderful occupation for retired politicians. The most famous garden in Su Chou was created by a Chinese Chancellor of the Exchequer, who built the Humble Administrator's garden while temporarily retired from politics. The Servant must recognize that to deceive others is often admirable but to deceive oneself is detestable: the myth and the Servant are secondary to the Idea. He must always remember this.

The Prince, the Idea and the Servant are the three legs of a stool; without any one of them, the stool will topple; each one is as important as the other, and each has its own distinct function. In *The Prince*, Machiavelli catches something of this when he directs that 'Princes should delegate to others the enactment of unpopular measures and keep in their own hands the distribution of favours.' This is the only sign in *The Prince* of a shared relationship between the Servant and the Prince. Over the centuries, Machiavelli has acquired a reputation for political cunning: in the popular mind 'Machiavellian behaviour' is associated with dirt, dishonesty and double-dealing. Although I recommend all of these in some form and more besides, I believe there is an essential nobility about the concept of the Prince, the Idea and the Servant working in unison. However dubious the means may look, this trinity fosters good government, and it is only when these three forces work together that nations can be governed with success. I do not claim that the failure of any one of these forces will destroy a nation, but I do claim that the effect of the three united, being a noble concept, will bring nobility to the state.

The whole object of this book is to show some of the devices that the Servant may deploy to help keep the Prince in power so he may carry out the Idea. The Servant's task is to see that nobody hinders the implementation of the Idea. This is not a handbook for those who would compromise. Quite the reverse: it would cast out trimmers of all sorts. Here you will find no easy advice or half measures, and acting on the information here will demand sacrifice. But the outcome can be triumph.

These notes on the conduct of the Servant are collected from many sources. For example, the relationship between the Prince and the Servant is not unlike the relationship between Mr Pickwick and Mr Sam Weller, a man who glorified in the concept of service, or between Bertie Wooster and Jeeves. Dickens and Wodehouse are not authors aspiring politicians normally go to for advice; but they could do worse.

The exercise of power is evident when everybody knows who has achieved a certain objective. The exercise of influence is when the same thing happens and nobody knows who has instigated it. Power is the declining state of a man who previously had influence. The Servant is a man of influence. If the Servant ever gives way to the temptation to exercise power, he can no longer serve and should be dismissed, for in the desire to exercise power, the Servant reveals an ambition to be the Prince. The Servant thereby also reveals his folly and his conceit, for he should know that it is much more satisfying to be influential than to be powerful. There is only one form of power that the Servant may, from time to time indulge in: the power to thwart the ambitions of others, or negative power. This is the most fun of all.

Whatever people's motives may appear to be, it is their real desires that matter. The Servant should not attempt to attribute motives to men's actions, for these are irrelevant. It is only actions that count. What future generations think of the motives of the Prince is likewise immaterial. The Servant lives for today, and he must use this fact to the advantage of the Prince. The Servant has no interest in the future, nor must he allow thoughts of how history will judge the Prince to influence his actions. He must also shape the past to suit the

[ 9 ]

Prince. Memories of other ages are recorded by historians who have scant regard for the evidence. These historians who try to please one group or another always distort the facts, which are further changed by fashion and politics over the years. This 'history' is then produced by men, like Machiavelli, as useful evidence for making decisions. The contemporary record of newspapers likewise becomes fact for historians, but, just as Hitler and Stalin rewrote history, so newspapers rewrite the present. The Prince, the Servant and their followers might just as well throw a handful of corn in the air and make decisions based on the shapes these seeds make when they fall to the ground. At least this will tell you which way the wind is blowing, and with what force. When making decisions, the Servant must reject history and the work of historians. History is useful only to the extent that it can justify actions the Prince has already decided upon.

In certain matters of fact – births, deaths, the outcome of battles – it would seem impossible to reinterpret history. For instance, it could not be argued that Napoleon won the Battle of Waterloo. However, it could be argued that it was either Blücher or Wellington who did win that battle. Even in great events there is scope for a particular interpretation. In smaller events the truth is often so obscure that even the people involved seldom know the actual truth, only the truth as they see it. Hence this becomes the perceived truth, and although it could be wrong, for all intents and purposes it is the truth. Most people believe the truth to be constant; in fact truth is what people believe. The Servant, knowing this, can create his own truths.

It is important to understand that an accepted fact is more powerful than the truth. Take miracles: the real truth is known only to God. The people who saw a miracle believe it; many people who did not see it do not believe it. The

Servant is not a seeker after absolute truth, but one who will take the view that best suits the Prince. The Servant will then promote that view until it becomes an established fact. As the argument moves away from the truth to the perceived truth, so the Servant has the evidence of his newly made 'facts' to base his argument on. Even though it may be far from the truth, the fact, once established, will be generally agreed by all. Thus it will seem a true fact as opposed to a false fact, or a lie. Let not the Servant base his argument on the laziness of a lie when true facts can be so easily summoned by his own skill.

Take the miracle of Fatima, which took place in Portugal in 1936. People saw, or believed that they saw, the sun spin towards the earth. Others believed that the laws of science cannot be suspended, and so disbelieved the miracle. Whether the miracle did in fact occur or not is of no consequence – it is how men believe that matters. Why disbelieve the eyewitness accounts of some, but believe those others who say that such an event is impossible? The truth is beyond the capacity of men to prove one way or the other. A miracle, like any event, will be believed and understood according to the way it is promoted.

Some men may challenge the assertions of the Servant, but when they do so they challenge what people generally believe. Unless they are engaged in folly they will not do this. This is why the Servant will not challenge the general views of the people, but rather use their views to base his arguments on. Old concepts can be powerful, and can provide a good base for the Idea, though they will never produce the Idea.

Machiavelli writes of a number of rulers who chose to murder their Servants once they had achieved power. Of course, it is very hard to employ anybody at all competent if you have a reputation for murdering them, and this is the stuff of fifteenth- and sixteenth-century Italy, but it does indicate that the Servant must consider very carefully the Prince whom he has helped to power. Consequently, the Servant must behave as if the time before his leader became the Prince does not exist. Sometimes Princes like to boast of their achievements to show just how far they have risen. When they do so, the Servant must never suggest that he helped in any way. Instead, the Servant might indicate to the newly established Prince that he was always a Prince in spirit, and that it was only a question of time before he became a Prince in name.

The Prince will know how to deal with established institutions. These are powerful forces; the Servant must realize this and treat their representatives with caution and courtesy, for in dangerous and complicated matters, there is no substitute for courtesy. This moves all kinds of people; never can there be too much courtesy in a Servant.

Recruits to the Idea must be made all the time. Sometimes the Servant will have to use his myth to make the Idea acceptable to those who resist it; the Servant will, with the help of the myth, obscure the Idea, but never will he attempt to change it. The Idea will always be clear to its true followers, but the support of fellow travellers is necessary, and if they do not fully understand what it is they are supporting, the Servant will just have to come to terms with that.

Machiavelli proposed simply to destroy all opposition after taking power, but that option does not work any longer amongst civilized peoples. It may yet apply to a few particularly selfish individuals, who can be destroyed by cunning rather than force, but it ought never to be tried on ideas. An idea is like certain plants; the more it is cut down, the stronger it becomes.

Nevertheless, the Servant must not allow himself to be put into a position where he appears to ally himself with any idea except the Prince's, for the Prince will feel jealous of other ideas and thus, by association, of the Servant himself. These other ideas fall into two categories: the active and the passive. For instance, religion is a passive idea: religion can coexist with other ideas; religion is not exclusive. It is important that while he does not himself become involved in it, the Servant treats religion with respect. (I include within religion ideas like the masonic movement, clubs and other men's associations.) It is vital that the Servant is not involved in situations where his emotional loyalty to the Prince may be tested, or where people think that by recruiting the Prince's Servant they have earned an advantage with the Prince. Treat all these organizations with courtesy; nothing more.

Other ideas, such as communism, socialism, conservatism, fascism and many more, are in this context active ideas: they are, or seek to be, exclusive of each other, and will be opposed by the Prince. He has his own Idea. The Servant must encourage and assist in the opposition of these ideas, for to oppose them with the Prince's own Idea, if done with vigour, can only make the Prince's Idea more vigorous. The Servant must attack these other ideas, although he must always show kindness and courtesy to their protagonists. This will be quite unexpected and will not be returned, thus ensuring that the Servant has the goodwill of disinterested observers. The Servant must be sure that he fully understands these opposing ideas. The Servant always learns before he acts and never attacks blindly.

Perhaps because he was an historian, Machiavelli advises the Prince to follow in the path of history, but history repeats itself only through an absence of originality in mankind. The Prince is unique and must be encouraged to think out problems afresh. After all, the Prince's enemies can read books as well. Originality should also be reflected in the way that the Servant carries out the Prince's plans. It is the Prince's Idea which will succeed or fail. If the Idea is strong enough, it can spread like morning mist. Without the Idea, no man can be the Prince. There will be times when the Idea is uncomfortable; then the Servant and his myth will have to play their full part.

The Prince, at times, may find that he has a great desire to be an ordinary man. However, Princes are not ordinary men, and under no circumstances must they be allowed to think that they are. It is the job of the Servant to reassure the Prince of that, constantly reminding him of his position. It may be that this desire of the Prince to be an ordinary man is brought about by an inclination to indulge in some of the vices of the ordinary man. This is unlikely in one who is truly the Prince; it is entirely possible, however, in one who would be the Prince, and in those who are born Princes it is almost certain, for they have an arrogance unique to their breeding. As far as he can, the Servant must observe and keep silent, hiding his knowledge even from the Prince. But he dare not let anyone else have access to this side of the Prince. The character of the people introduced to the Prince must never interfere with the running of the state. A Servant who arranges these things lives with fear. If the Servant has to become involved, then he must have well prepared his myth, for he will surely need it; nothing must be allowed to jeopardize the Idea.

There is a device that the Servant may find useful from time to time; that device is called the 'false accusation'. The Servant encourages his enemies to accuse him of some discreditable action or other, preferably the sort of action that the Servant clearly has no desire to commit. The Servant then allows all and sundry to believe that he is guilty. At the moment when the enemies of the Servant are celebrating the great currency achieved by their accusation, forgetting all other things of which they might accuse the Servant, it is proved by physical circumstances that the Servant could not possibly be guilty. The enemies of the Servant are discredited and it is hard, even impossible for them to accuse him of other misdeeds. This device of the mistaken accusation has been the salvation of more than one guilty man.

The Prince will have around him ministers who are both capable and cunning. All these men are rivals of the Prince and, since they know the Servant to have the ear of the Prince and wish to remain on friendly terms, will only tell him what they want the Prince to hear. These men cannot all be destroyed, but one of them should be posted to some unruly province or place with an uncertain future, as an example on which the others can reflect.

These rivals will try to persuade the Prince to move away from his Idea so that they can destroy the Prince and succeed him. The Prince must not be driven from his Idea or he will fall, and as he falls, so will the Servant. The Servant's job is to hinder, both in secret and in public, through the use of strategies and technicalities, any attempt to change the Idea. The whole reason for his service lies in the preservation of the Idea and the Prince.

The problem facing the Prince is how to promote his Idea, control his colleagues and at the same time make the population happy. The Idea, if it remains pure, will be too strong for potential dissenters, for colleagues will not desert an Idea that is operating successfully for one that is not. They may aspire to be Princes, but they are mere soldiers. They will desert when they think that the Idea has become so devalued as to become indistinguishable from others. The people may then wonder if, in practice, the Idea is really to their benefit and grow to dislike it. In this case their emotions must be tapped by the Prince, who in his preaching of the Idea must reject any suggestion of doubt.

The Servant must cultivate his myth. He does this by appearing in a variety of personalities to a variety of carefully chosen people, then making certain that, at the right time, all these people meet. The result is confusion and, as people prefer order, they will invent a larger, more complex personality for him – based on the evidence that the Servant has given to each of them. This personality the Servant may then adjust before spreading it, and developing his myth. Without it, he will be just another official of the court. It goes without saying that the Servant must be a man of competence, but however competent he may be, all will be lost without the myth. It need have no connection with reality; the Servant can be naturally cruel or kind; it will make no difference provided he attends to his myth. The myth of the Servant must never be confused with the Idea of the Prince, which is his alone.

The Servant deals in controlled confusion. He allows people to believe their own inventions about his life and background by using people who are in the habit of gossiping. He will let carefully placed disinformation build up a picture in their minds. When some say evil he will find others who will say only good of him, and out of this contradiction the Servant will take those parts that he needs in the construction of his myth, and have them repeated by men of authority in matters of gossip. So one man will say to another, 'I know this man; he is clearly this or that. I can tell you this in confidence.' And the man to whom he says these things will say, 'You make a great mistake when you say this about the Servant. I happen to know the truth.' And this one will repeat what he has been told, because men can always be relied upon to repeat matters that they are told in confidence. Soon these things about the Servant will be written down, and will become the perceived truth – which is known to be very far from the truth.

Most of his battles will be fought quietly, for that is how the Servant prefers to influence actions: by changing the order in which events happen, for example, so that opponents discover that what they oppose has altered, though they find it hard to identify how. In open warfare, however, the myth of the Servant requires a degree of aggression, possibly a little crudity. This is what people expect in warfare, and the myth of the Servant should always be predictable. In peacetime, the myth depends on his kindness and sympathy, for this is the nature of peace, and thus, predictable. While the appearance of predictability is important, this should not imply that the Servant himself cannot be flexible in practice. It is the Servant's myth that is predictable.

The Servant must have assistants who will stay with him long enough to know how he works, but not too long. A good employee will probably take five years to rise, and then have five years at his best, followed by five years of decline when his energy is beginning to fail. All those who would hold a high position should remember that it is in the last years that they will be most loved, since people tend to love and respect those who, having been many years in the same post, do not have much longer to serve. The Servant knows this – and he knows that it is the prospect of their going that the people love.

The Servant must give credit for his rise as often as he can to others, and attribute any successes he may have to these men. Often they will be men of little account, so the Servant will construct legends about them to advance their prestige.

The Servant must be a good judge of men and how they will behave. This is a difficult art, as we are all inclined to see other men in the light that suits us. The Servant does not need to judge men's talents so much as spot the changes in them. Even a physical alteration in a man – a loss of weight, a new style of dress – may indicate a change in his actions, and can serve as a warning to the Servant. Other changes may vary from the need to create to the desire to destroy, from the need to work to the wish to laze. They happen for many reasons, but the Servant need know only that men do change, and how to discern this. Men will often create circumstances to precipitate change, or manufacture incidents after the event to justify their new position.

In the matter of the truth and the perceived truth, there is no single truth about men, but the perceived truth is the operative truth, for this is what people see and believe. What men know and believe about themselves is impossible to tell, but it is probably very distant from the truth: most men will believe what they want to believe. The Servant does not deal with men as they are, but as they think they are. He, on the other hand, has carefully and knowingly constructed a myth for himself. Because it is constructed with great care, the Servant can distinguish between the truth and the myth.

As I have said, there will be occasions, in the service of the Prince and the Idea, when events are so dire that the Servant has to take action that disregards his myth. By doing so he will startle and disturb people who are always angered by inconsistency. Such a change of character may also surprise his enemies, though this must not be relied upon. An avenue of retreat, such as a temporary sickness, must become a component of the myth. This will reveal a human weakness, a quality for which people will have sympathy – as long as the battle is eventually joined and won. When using sickness as an excuse, make it truly revolting. This will be believed and will avoid discussion. Men do not lightly enter into talk of each other's bowels.

The Servant must also embrace the myths of strength and of clemency. These have to be deployed carefully, without showing signs of weakness. In reality, the Servant is ruthless, not letting kindness or consideration enter into his plans. This is the paradox of his position. In the area where the line between the man and the myth is drawn, there can be no blurring of the edges between stealth and action, honesty and cunning, kindness and cruelty, generosity and meanness. Not to draw the line will destroy the concept of the Servant, and unless he is dismissed, he will bring down the Prince.

In the usual course of events one man succeeds another, often someone who has died. Most people respect someone who is dead, even though he was capable of doing them harm and was not popular while he lived. This might appear to be a disadvantage to a Prince and his Servant, but the Servant ensures that the Prince can absorb the respect felt for his predecessor, slowly drawing strength from his popularity while actually consuming it until it seems enclosed by the Prince and his Idea. If this predecessor's popularity was in doubt, the Servant may contrast the Prince's own Idea with it, showing the Prince's Idea to be superior to the actions or policies of his predecessor.

The Servant's dilemma is that he must be feared as a man of authority, while simultaneously he must be loved for the attractive qualities of his person. By love, I mean the love of the populace and not the other, more dangerous emotion that people bestow on others in order to bind them to their own desires and ambitions. I mean respect. The Servant must never believe that anybody really loves or respects him, not even the Prince. All they see and believe is but his myth. All men need reassurance and find public expression of these emotions very attractive. The Servant must, in his own mind, reject the lure of popularity; he is there only to serve the Prince and the Idea. The only publicity sought by the Servant, then, must be for the promotion of his myth, not to acquire the love of the population. He must always remember that he has only one role, that is to serve. His strength and self-respect must come from that, and that alone.

The Servant must, in all things he does, display great confidence; but not arrogance or the sort of presumption that leaves suspicion in men's minds. Privately, he must have no confidence. He must plan carefully, never relying on the promises of others, and his plan must never assume success. There must always be emergency measures to fall back on. The myth of the Servant will differ between those who are close and fear his position, and those who are distant and love and respect him. The latter make their judgements on the smallest amount of evidence. The former, because they are close, are more selective, and may know enough to begin to doubt the myth. The Servant should employ a person to administer discipline among his staff. When this person has become too objectionable, he can be given other duties.

The Servant must be conscious of personal ambition. He knows full well about this, for he is the sort of man who, in any other role, would be consumed by the desire for success. It would be the driving force of his life. His colleagues would admire this ambition, and be jealous of it and, if he failed, they would say of him that he was too ambitious. The Servant must understand that he no longer has an ambition because he has achieved it. By making himself essential to the Prince, he has reached the pinnacle of his career. Since there is nowhere to promote him, he is beyond ambition. The Prince will feel secure because the Servant is not a rival, and when the Idea begins to prosper it will be to their mutual benefit.

None the less, ambition can prove troublesome. The Prince will be treated by people as a prince, while the Servant will be treated as a servant. The Servant will be tempted to use his skill to prove to these people that he is really the equal of a Prince. This is one of the tests of a Servant, for he must be satisfied by the knowledge that he is part of a trinity, and ignore those who would make trouble. The Servant must never indulge in petty actions to prove his status. He needs all the qualities of the ambitious – the driving force and the courage – but must never demonstrate that he has fulfilled his goal. The Servant himself knows this. There is no need for anyone else to know.

It is the job of the Servant to be the Praetorian Guard of the Prince, to be always alert. He will have time for pleasure, but will take his pleasure in activities where he meets men who can be of help to him in his task, for he must devote every hour to the Prince. Only by keeping constantly in mind the Idea of the Prince can the Servant perform his task. He must have his own network of informants and men who will assist him. He must always know how to use the network of the state. Since this network is unlikely to be loyal to the Prince, it must be used with great care, and never trusted.

Information must be gathered by employing a large number of skilled men to assemble background information on a wide variety of subjects. The Servant should thus always be able to make an informed judgement as to the likely turn of events. The Servant listens to many men, weighing their words before reaching his own conclusion. Paid informers must never be used; if by chance the Servant comes across a seller of information, he should be listened to and paid for his services, but these men should never be sought out. Men who sell information for money, ambition or revenge must never be believed in total, although there is an element of truth in every lie, and the best lies are often based on the truth. The words of honest men should always be respected but not totally believed either, for honest men often exaggerate to lend credibility to their truths. The question for the Servant is not whether the messenger is reliable, but who has sent the message, and why. Stupid men are the most dangerous because they may try to make a message more interesting, and they will deliver it incorrectly, causing confusion. The Servant must listen to idle gossip, taking a word from here and picking a word from there, always checking, always looking for a pattern.

The Prince must always be seen to keep faith. This is a very difficult task to perform and may not always be possible, but since the Prince and the Idea are the same, the Idea can only be damaged by any duplicity. There are, therefore, two possibilities: firstly, the Servant tries to prevent the Prince making promises that he may find difficult to keep; the second is that, in the event of a pledge being broken, the Servant must arrange for someone else to take the blame. It makes no difference whether the Servant himself is honest or dishonest, although the myth must suggest honesty. The Servant must be able to change quickly, or quicker than events. When setting out on a strategy of deceit, he must choose very carefully who he will deceive, for while honest men will see the Servant as honest, a deceitful man will spot the Servant's deceit. It is in the nature of men, when looking at others, to see themselves, and apply their own values. Dealing in deceit, as the Servant must, great caution is required. The Servant should know the difference between large and small deceits. Avoid small deceits: like barnacles on the bottom of a ship, they build up in the minds of people whom you may need to convince in a large deceit, making the task harder, sometimes impossible. Avoid deceit when possible – let men deceive themselves, for usually they will believe what they choose to believe. Show them only an easy way, an option that will enhance their prestige and their wealth, and most men will invent their own deceits. Honest men are more difficult, but many of them would rather avoid the issue. They do not need to be deceived, only shown a reason for looking the other way. But beware the exceptional man, the man of conviction, for he could be a Prince.

While the Servant and those close to the Prince will be motivated by the Prince's Idea, others will be moved only by reward. The Servant must ensure that the further these men are from the Prince, the greater their opportunity for reward is, for they are capable of weakening the Idea. From time to time it is the Servant's job to indicate to certain distant but key figures that there is a chance of plunder, so that they continue to work hard for the Prince.

Princes, like many other people, do not like advice unless it coincides with their own thoughts. If the Servant anticipates the Prince's wishes and advises him accordingly, he becomes just another flatterer, an ornament in a court. If you wish to win his respect, do not advise the Prince; make yourself indispensable instead. Seek to remove trivial problems, help him avoid more serious problems. Never ask for guidance. Princes have enough decisions to make already. Never draw his attention to the fact that you perform this role. He will notice. A Prince badly in need of advice is not one to serve. The success of the Servant lies in his choice of Prince; he must choose carefully his Prince. It is the only choice he makes.

What the Prince needs is evidence on which to make decisions. It is the job of the Servant to provide it. In assessing the Prince's judgement, there is a single criterion: does the Prince have all the evidence, and does the Servant know everything that the Prince knows? The Servant never disagrees, just provides the missing evidence. It is, of course, the Servant who grades the worth of the evidence.

The Servant will never acknowledge that his judgement is better than that of the Prince. If the Prince makes a mistake and events prove the Servant's judgement to have been right, the Servant should say nothing. An unwise Servant who gave advice which led to a mistake would damage his position; a Servant who gave correct advice that was neglected would find his relationship with the Prince damaged. If the mistake is fatal, all is lost; if it is only a setback, then the Servant must help to recover the situation. Since he gave no advice, his capacity to serve will be undamaged. If the Prince is continually making mistakes, this is not the Prince to serve, for it seems that he was never truly a Prince. The Prince is not to blame, however, if the Servant foresaw a mistake, and by exercising influence could have stopped it and did not. If the Servant cannot influence without advising, he is a failure as a Servant. If these mistakes eventually cause the Prince to fall, this is an indication of the Servant's lack of ability to serve, support and guide the Prince.

It is the balance of trust between the Prince and his Servant that will make their partnership flourish or founder, and this subtle balance is most likely to be affected by small events. The control of this balance is the job of the Servant. The Servant must be capable of independent thought. It is important for the Prince to know of this, but equally vital that the Servant never exhibits his independence of thought on issues of wider policy. Here the Servant never needs to exercise independent thought, for he must serve only the Idea.

Princes are impressed by wealth. They conclude from the fact that the Servant has wealth that he is clever and that he could leave when he disagreed with them. They will also believe that if the Servant has wealth, he is likely to be honest and not to steal. The Prince will also conclude that the Servant is lucky, and above all else Princes like to be served by lucky men. Because the Prince must not believe the Servant to be extremely clever, far better that he believes him to be lucky.

The Servant must be well travelled, so when foreign places are discussed he can provide background information. He must know many people, particularly the Prince's political contemporaries. He must take a deep interest in the minutiae of their lives, again to give background information. He must be cunning, but never plot. His private life does not have to be straightforward, though it is preferable that he conforms to the morals of the age. Those who would attack a Prince through the morals of his Servant expose their hand to little purpose because, to serve well, the Servant must always recognize that he is dispensable in the service of the Prince. It is preferable that the Servant appears to live an open life and allows his failings to be well known. These are part of his myth, so that if they are attacked, they are not a shock to anyone. And being part of his myth, they can easily be got rid of. Bachelors make better Servants because they have more time, and their actions are not influenced by their wives. It helps if his contemporaries think a Servant is lazy, amiable and not too clever. A fullness of figure helps sustain this disguise. The Prince will see through it. With the Prince the

Servant must be amusing, so that he will wish to have his Servant constantly near him.

The Servant must display his wealth to the Prince with prudence, and should never let the Prince see his home. When Cardinal Wolsey and Fouché, both men of wealth and taste, did this, the result was disaster. In both cases the Prince that they served became extremely jealous. In the case of Cardinal Wolsey, his Prince believed that he could have afforded such magnificence only by dishonesty, and that such dishonesty must be to the Prince's disadvantage. In fact he believed that his Servant had at best used his name to rob others, at worst robbed him personally. This suspicion terminated their relationship, or at least it gave the Prince the chance to rid himself of one who perhaps had grown too close. In the case of Fouché, his Prince threw him into jail charged with dishonesty; perhaps his real reason was jealousy of Fouché's mansion, Vaux le Vicomte, even though this Prince built Versailles and is remembered as the Sun King. All those who have visited Vaux le Vicomte will recall the great good taste of Fouché, but in the end that was his downfall. The Servant must never outshine the Prince. Only the Idea can compete with the Prince, and so the myth of the Servant must be a humble myth. The Servant is content with this humble myth, for he knows the true greatness of service is made all the greater by the importance of the Prince. The Servant must gain nothing from his service. There must be no suggestion that the Servant profits from his employment; unlike morality, this could bring down both the Servant and the Prince. Let this wealth of yours be part of the myth, a demonstration of a style of life. Be not rich if the Prince sees you as poor; appear not poor if the Prince believes you rich.

The Servant should use a little of his wealth to pay a few retainers. These are his own appointments, and not an extension of the patronage of the state or his master. These men should be retired from the game of politics, drawn from the press or party, but not the machinery of state. They will be grateful to be involved at all, and not ask too high a reward. These men are the Servant's tentacles, and will provide the first warning of an attack. They must not be relied upon for defence, but only to serve as warning posts.

The Servant will see that the Prince has enough money to fight battles, though this must be dedicated to fighting his own battles, not those of the people who provided the money. The Servant must prevent the Prince from becoming a mercenary. Of course, it is true that the money for war must be raised in peacetime. When he need offer his supporters nothing but his friendship, then the Prince is truly a Prince. But men often wish to exact a price from a Prince who is under threat.

The dilemma facing the Servant is that the people who pay to meet Princes are not the sort of people that Princes should meet. This is where the Servant's knowledge of commerce is useful. A Servant who, although practised in the art of service, is a failure in the world of business, brings with him the wrong connections and is likely to be brought down, or at least brought into disrepute. Nor is it the job of a Servant to suggest to a Prince who he should associate with; this is part of a Prince's judgement. The Servant's role is to make certain people available to the Prince. If the Prince likes their company, so much the better. The identity of these people will depend on why the Servant wishes them to meet the Prince, whether for information, for advice or for pleasure. They must stick to their role. If they move out of it, they must be separated from the Prince. The Servant must never do this himself, but there are various techniques, such as alerting one of the Prince's advisers on to whose ground this person has strayed. His jealousy aroused, the adviser will do the rest.

The Servant must be totally ruthless, even if he prefers his myth to suggest that he is not. He carries out the wishes of the Prince; he has none of his own. The Servant's power is the power of his personality. He must be able to persuade people to take actions against their will, and must have the tenacity to see that they carry them out. On no account should the Servant threaten them with the power of the state. The power of the state and the wrath of the Prince are the Prince's prerogative, and only his.

The Servant I describe is unusual as Servants go. He is not simply hired or fired. He is not employed for just one purpose. He does not stay on when masters change, nor does he leave on a whim, for personal reasons, or for other trivia. People who do these things can be intermittently useful to a Prince, but I write of a man of business, a true Servant, a man close to the Prince and yet distant, a man to be used, but used only with care. The man of business is the confidential Servant, always in possession of information that could destroy his master. Yet the Servant can never use this knowledge to further his ambitions. To do so would force the Prince to destroy him, for the delicate balance between the Prince and the Servant would be upset. Never threaten Princes. The Servant may think like a Prince, but never act like one. Servants do not stand for election; they are appointed by their master, they serve only him. In defeat they follow that master and work for his return. The Servant owes responsibility only to his Prince and the Prince's Idea; to the state the Servant owes nothing, for the state will only benefit from the success of the Prince's Idea. The responsibility of the state is the Prince's burden, and the Servant makes no judgement in this matter. Once committed, the Servant must carry out only the Prince's will, regardless of his own view.

Machiavelli said that the trouble with Servants (whom he described as mercenaries) is that they are lazy and dangerous. Their laziness occurs when they do not wish to fight, and the danger stems from their ambition. The Servant can overcome the first part of this indictment by diligence. In politics the greatest talent is stamina; the ability to be there, to attend, because to be available at the right moment means being there at all the moments; the habit of attending endless boring meetings, being there at the beginning, waiting until the end, being there at all times, being always available. The Prince, though, will judge the Servant lazy only if he fails. In success, laziness is irrelevant. As for courage in the face of an enemy, who knows who has that? In a crisis, the Servant must carry out the Prince's instructions to the letter. Independent thought is not called for in a crisis; it can unbalance a plan and in these circumstances prove totally disastrous. The Servant has no other role at these times but to be the arm of his master. Other members of the court, relatives, princelings, friends, clowns, dressers, spokesmen and petty officials imagine that they are there to help, and often try to do so without the knowledge of the Prince. This is the real danger, for if these courtiers have talent, their actions will be unco-ordinated and competitive, and if they are fools, they will confuse the Prince, especially if they unwittingly chance upon the right course of action.

Machiavelli's observation that the talent of hirelings might make them dangerous must be taken very seriously by the Servant, for again it touches on the possibility of jealousy. It is always possible for the Prince to become jealous of a successful Servant. The Servant can overcome this danger by presenting himself to the Prince as a specialist, appearing to be expert in one major area in order to have access to the Prince's thoughts on many other subjects. But in order to remain close to the Prince, the Servant must also be adept at fulfilling a thousand small tasks, because small needs are frequent.

In order to establish in the Prince's mind that the Servant is a specialist, it is important for him to comment only on his subject, and to assert, when asked of other matters, 'I know too little to be of help.' The parafanatics of the court (those who are fanatical about the paraphernalia of the court, men who invest all their energies in insisting upon the observance of protocol, men who care not who the Prince is, being interested only in presence and position and not the Idea) will give advice on any matter. The Prince, seeing the Servant's limitations and knowing his own supreme talent (for he is a Prince), will not fear the Servant as a rival or feel jealousy towards him. The parafanatics will not try to destroy the Servant, for he does not compete for the Prince's ear against their desires or advice. These other advisers are more often interested in giving advice than in carrying through the actions that flow from it. Eventually, the constant Servant is in a position to influence the Prince on subjects on which he says he knows too little to be of help.

The Servant must be very careful not to form alliances in the name of the Prince. Only the Prince himself may make these connections, and, however tempting an alliance may seem, the Servant must avoid this. To make an alliance is to incur a debt that may become embarrassing to repay, for, if the Prince does not do so, it will weaken both the Servant and the Prince.

Better not to create opportunities for men who may become enemies. These men should have honour heaped on them, for this will discredit them among their fellows. Whatever they think of the Prince, it is hard to criticize a generous nature. These men, if they do criticize the Prince after they have accepted his generosity, will lack credibility with all except the Prince's bitterest enemies.

The Servant knows that he will have no reward and that in the end he will sacrifice himself for his master. That *is* his reward, and that is the nature of the Servant. But on leaving the Prince, other members of the staff must be highly rewarded. Indeed, in the view of others, they should be too highly rewarded. This will please them, and they will speak well of the Prince, although this should not be counted on, and it will cause others to be jealous of them, and ensure that they cannot rally support against the Prince should their loyalty fail. The scale of their reward will encourage their successors.

In a true Servant there is no discontent. A disgruntled Servant should not even begin to serve the Prince, for it is from service that the Servant draws his pride (although this pride must remain hidden). When the Prince gives the Servant a task, it is for him to carry it out without hesitation. Should anything go wrong, the Servant will take the blame. When it goes right the Prince will receive the praise.

The Servant does not even think about a plan until he is certain of the Prince's wishes. Since Princes seldom give direct instructions, it is vital that the Servant is in total sympathy with the Prince, for he must be able to read his mind. Great Princes like to plan great strategies, but they do not like to be asked to make small decisions. When the Servant is sure of the Prince's intentions, he should plan quickly and act with speed. Never hesitate, for even Princes are indiscreet. Never even conceive a plan till it is needed: even as you read the Prince's mind, others will be watching you. If you already have a plan in mind, it can be betrayed by decisions you take that are influenced by knowledge you have and others do not.

The Prince will make only one judgement: 'Did you succeed?' If 'Yes', expect no reward. If 'No', you misread his mind and may have to be sacrificed. Princes come to power in a variety of ways. If your Prince has been brought to power by others who are unknown to you, those who did not get the positions that they sought will seethe with disappointment. The Servant must sympathize with them and extend just a little hope. To those who are chosen, he should fire their ambition slightly, always recalling that success comes only from the Prince. The Servant will find out about the Prince's appointments a little in advance and speak to the recipients in such a way that, when they hear the news, they will believe that since the Servant knew these things already he must have had a hand in them.

The Prince will try to balance the power among his followers; the Servant should never seek to unbalance it.

The Prince can also be brought to power by others, out of revenge. These plotters are going to expect him to be 'their' Prince. This is, of course, not possible. A true Prince is accountable to his Idea and to the people who follow his Idea, *not* to miscellaneous conspirators. In time, these frustrated people will try to overthrow the Prince, for they will have used him to remove a Prince that they did not care for and now wish to have a Prince who will carry out only their ideas. If they do not succeed, they will turn on the Servant. Like angry animals they will seek revenge; all the actions of the Prince will be blamed on the Servant, and these people will call for his dismissal. The dismissal of the Servant is the first step towards the dismissal of the Prince and the destruction of the Idea. In the meantime, the Servant must get to know them well, smile at them and accumulate information about them.

The Servant must also see that none of their assistants occupies any role in the Prince's party. These people have to be removed slowly, in advance of an attack on the Prince. Do not underestimate the role of the minor figures: the Servant must always remember that men will sacrifice more for revenge than they will for gain. The Servant must see that the Prince does not casually put them into a position where they can exact the desired revenge. They are frustrated and must be heaped with honour and wealth (though not power), so that when they attack the Prince, they are seen by the population to be graceless. But these are supposed to be the Prince's friends. What of his known political enemies?

Besides the entrenched opposition, there are the supporters of other Princes who may be persuaded to share the Idea. The Servant must detach as many of them as he can. The Prince must never alter his Idea, for it is the currency of his office, but the Servant can present it in a way that will appeal to these men because they are essentially mercenaries. Once detached, they may be used, but never relied on.

But if the Servant is able to move a man from entrenched opposition to the Prince's Idea, to support the Prince in his Idea, this is a prize indeed. I speak later about converts in general, but occasionally one or two of these converts should be given high office, for he can never return from whence he came and will therefore be secure and loyal to the Prince, until he has some new Idea to follow. These men must not be neglected.

Both the Prince and the Servant have a role in the business of winning new supporters. The Prince expresses the Idea and the Servant promotes it. All Servants have rivals, and they will take care that, in eliminating a rival, the power of another is not increased, or a new threat established. When a rival rises in the Prince's favour, the Servant ought to take a relaxed view; events are never as serious as they seem. Tread with care. Do not enter into battle with this rival; the Servant must repudiate jealousy; there is always the chance of losing much for only a little gain. If this rival has to be dealt with, always remember that all rivals have rivals of their own. Suggest quietly to one of these that he may care to deal with his rival.

The Prince must never be asked to fight the Servant's battles; indeed, it is best if the Servant does not fight his own battles. He must find others to fight his battles for him. Should a number of rivals combine to attack the Servant, this is a different matter, for this amounts to an attack on the Prince himself. This must be brought swiftly to his notice, for he needs to know of the danger to himself. This is a battle that the Prince will fight, for it is in truth his own battle.

In the early days of the Prince's rule, the Servant should indicate his support for the old order in his party or faction. This will infuriate certain radicals and cause them to join his rivals. They will then try to overcome the Servant; the old order will join the fight on the Servant's side, for they hate these radicals. Curtailing the activities of the radicals is useful to the Prince too, for, helpful as they may have been, he now governs all the people, and any elaboration of the Idea must be done by him, and him alone. The Prince will resent radicals advancing the Idea for their own purposes.

When the Prince is established, the old order must disappear gradually, for fear it compromise the Idea by watering it down. Some of the radicals must be encouraged to return to the fold, and become supporters again, believing that the Prince has by now developed his Idea to their satisfaction. The role of these selected radicals changes over time. To begin with, they will have joined with the old order to destroy the rivals of the Prince and the Servant; then, as the old order seems still to hold too much power, they will ally with the Prince finally to destroy it. The new order thus created soon becomes the old order.

Sometimes the Servant will have served the Prince before he attained his rank. It is in the nature of some Princes to want grander men as their Servants when they come to power. Some actually worry about Servants who knew them in humbler times. In early days the Servant must move carefully, indicating how his prestige increases with that of the Prince. Yet the Servant must not allow his myth to become too grand; the Servant himself is far from grand.

As the Prince will have need of company, the Servant may arrange for the great people of the last regime to be introduced. These grandees who formerly opposed the Prince should be used to ornament the Prince's court, without ever being seen as ornaments. Their advice should be often sought, and the Servant must indicate to the world that their advice is always taken by the Prince. In fact the Prince should never take their advice, but since it has been given privately and its content is known only to the Prince and the ornament in question, no one else will know whether it has been followed or not. But these ornaments, hearing that the Prince always takes their advice, will be flattered and believe that he has. So pleased will they be, that they will tell everyone that the Prince follows their advice, and will be seen to be allies of the Prince. But the Servant will know the truth.

When the Prince comes to power, he will find that powerful groups of men who believed that they were responsible for getting him there now expect him to rule according to their instructions. The Prince must find a way to deal with these men, and with their policies, for both are serious matters. Men can be removed only by promotion: their lot must be improved. There is no single way to deal with these people. Some may undergo a conversion. These men are reliable for the moment, as they have nowhere to go. But over time beware these men, they are unsteady, they could become the Prince's strongest critic. Having nothing but the Idea, they feel a passion for it, and perhaps jealousy of the Prince whose Idea it is. Maybe it is better to introduce other passions into the lives of these men. The Servant must reflect on this; some will be promoted to positions of great honour and little consequence; some will have to be sent off to do other work (the Servant must find occupations for them). The removal of these men from any influence on the Idea is essential; only those who truly believe in it must be allowed near the Idea. The Servant is the guardian of the Idea; the Prince invents and propagates the Idea. During this period, the Servant's job is to see that the Prince is not bothered by trivia.

This is the time when the Prince sets the style for his whole rule. He comes under great pressure to change the Idea. He will be tempted to please both those that remain from old regimes and also the population. He will be offered many easy alternatives to the Idea, and many good reasons for adopting them, and he will not find it hard to persuade himself that courses other than the one he has chosen are best. As it succeeds the Idea will, of course, evolve – what sort of an idea would it be if it did not? One doomed to failure. But it will evolve as events evolve, change slowly to deal with circumstances that have occurred, and in this world of truth and perceived truth the Idea should change only according to the truth. The Idea must not be changed according to the views of those who would use it for convenience, people who would change the Idea for they fear this and they fear that. There must be good reason and good evidence for considering the adaptation of the Idea; the Idea must not be changed lightly, and the guardians of the Idea must be determined men.

Moreover, having won power, the Prince will wish to enjoy it and to have no unpleasantness around him. The Prince will be subjected to many trivial pleasures; societies previously closed to him will be opened, he will be in a position to help those that he has always shown an interest in. Beware of this, Servant, and direct the Prince to serious matters, dealing with these trivialities yourself. Jealousy is the danger that comes with new favourites; if there is to be jealousy it must be blamed on the Servant, not on the Prince; the Servant, using his myth, knows how to avoid this blame. But the Prince has not gained power for its own sake. He has gained power to implement the Idea, and the Servant's job is to help in the implementation of the Idea. The Servant must encourage him to stick firmly to it. He will play no active part in deciding how to deal with the great matters of policy, although he will take a keen interest in observing who does.

When the new Prince comes to power, the Servant should act as if the Prince always had it. Because Princes, whether elected or hereditary, have an inborn capacity to govern. It is the quality that the Servant chooses to follow. It is important that the Prince knows this.

I have spoken before of senior officials who help the Prince to power and expect employment. Now I speak of smaller figures. Some will receive jobs, while some will be disappointed. The Servant invents roles for these minor figures, because the Prince has no time to consider them, and they cannot recommend themselves. These lesser figures, while they are no threat to the Prince, could cause the Servant trouble and thus hinder his ability to serve the Prince. He should find positions for these small men outside the world of politics, among the many jobs that are in the gift of the Prince and his followers.

The Servant will find them jobs with small salaries and great prestige. In the world of the arts, for example, or among the many committees of the great institutions of the state. Small men, such as writers of popular books or tunes, may be allowed to attend upon the Prince, since they will amuse him. That is their talent, and it is most unlikely that they would be chosen to replace the Servant, so he need have no fear of them. These small men often have great conceit, particularly the writers of popular books. Their own ambition knowing no bounds, these men believe the Servant's role to be a humble role; they believe that the Servant is merely one who fetches and carries for a Prince. They have no understanding of the grandeur of service, and cannot see that serving a great Prince is a role that gives great personal satisfaction. They seek jobs far greater than that of the Servant, and the spectacle is very humorous. These men seek fame for themselves, and have no interest in the Prince beyond this. These men would not know an idea if they lived for a millennium, far less discover one for themselves. These men seek only grand roles with grand titles so that all will see how grand they are, and even then they will pretend to be grander still. These men are fools: all courts must have fools, and their folly must be encouraged by the Servant. The Prince will believe that the things they say are to entertain him, for no sane man would believe them to be true. These foolish men can be extremely useful for they like to talk at length, and their talking can occupy the time of the Prince, empty time that might otherwise be filled by troublemakers. These foolish men are entertainment, and exist only to entertain.

After this first period of his rule, the Prince tires of this amusement, and such people will fade. The Servant will be secure again, without having had the trouble of removing these people himself, and without the irritation that might have been caused should they have been removed roughly.

Machiavelli observes that Princes, especially new ones, tend to find more loyalty among those men whom they originally distrusted than among those whom they trusted. The Idea converts enemies into allies, and by rewarding these converts the Prince encourages others. It is true that the whole point of politics is to change men's minds, and as I have said a few of these men are suitable for high office – but it is doubtful, although they show the true zeal of converts, whether they can be trusted fully. True, they cannot return whence they came; they cannot be rivals. It would seem therefore that, in general, they are the ideal courtiers. But it must never be forgotten that they have been political enemies and may, in time, turn dangerous again for any one of a thousand irrational reasons. However they may rationalize their change, the fact that they made it in the first place shows them to be irrational and so dangerous. The Servant must find other matters to fill the minds of these men. Never allow them to become courtiers; ensure their lives are occupied with other activities so that they will have no desire to be courtiers. For such converts must not feel the frustration of isolation from the Prince and the Idea, both of whom they now love. These are dangerous men.

As to the treatment of the loyal old supporters, it is not in the nature of the Prince to neglect them. If they begin to fail due to an inability to adapt to the Prince in power, he will simply shift their functions to someone else, while leaving them with the title and all the trappings of the job. The Prince will continue to praise them, and the Servant will go on encouraging them.

The servants of former leaders must be treated with respect and, although they have failed, they must be promoted. This makes them useless to their former employers, who will be jealous of them. The Prince should never feel the need to destroy a former leader's servants, or even former leaders themselves. Always offer promotion: deal more than generously with former leader's servants and former leaders, for if they reject the promotion that is offered and that promotion is seen to be generous, then they will be regarded as churlish, and do what they will, say what they will, thus treated there is no possibility that they can blame the Idea or the Prince.

The Prince destroys old ideas with his Idea. Former leaders must be given great honour and raised above the battle. Having grown accustomed to this style of life, they will not risk it for the sake of younger men and frustrated men who work on new ideas. Let these former Princes continue to preach the defeated idea. If you leave an old cockerel in a pen of chickens, you will not get many fertile eggs. He may have become infertile, but the young cocks are still no match for him. Better still, the radical young men will be discouraged by the former leaders and their servants who are now enjoying these honours. It makes current allies out of former rivals. There is little danger in the defeated idea, but great menace in a new idea. Let the old ideas suffocate new ideas. The Prince should not allow himself to be blamed for resisting the new men and their idea. By doing so, the Prince will only draw attention to their virtues.

The Servant must cut off any avenue of retreat for the supporters of the Prince, committing them utterly to the Idea. The Servant must also see that there is nowhere for the Prince to go should he be tempted to leave his Idea. The Prince must stay with his Idea, and any retreat from it alters his relationship with the Servant and destroys the point of this relationship. The Idea, having grown stronger because of its consistency, will attract supporters and, when it comes under attack, they will defend it.

The Idea will also attract supporters who, while not particularly caring for the Idea itself, so dislike the opponents who are attacking the Prince that they support his Idea. These men must be watched, for when times are hard they will advise that compromise is necessary. There is no harm in adjusting the empirics of the Idea, but the Idea, although it can evolve, must never be changed for convenience. If they are taken seriously, all will be lost, for ever. There will be times when the Prince is very unpopular. The Servant must encourage the Prince to reaffirm his Idea at these moments, for popularity is never universal or constant. The Prince's Idea is not about popularity; the Servant must always remember that the population distrust change, and to change the Idea at a moment of crisis, even if it were momentarily sensible to do so, would prove fatal, even if this course of action did succeed. If the Prince survives only by weakening his Idea, by trimming or compromising around the edges of the Idea, or by actions of convenience, he will as surely bring down the Idea as if he had torn out its heart.

When the regime changes, it is vital that all the old retainers of that regime are dealt with honourably. This costs the new Prince nothing, although it does make the beneficiaries the objects of the jealousy of his own supporters. Consequently, a Prince must not take them into his confidence, because this will unsettle his supporters. They must be honoured publicly and cast out in private, so that when they complain, as they will, they seem ungracious. If you propose to destroy a possible enemy, do so by promoting him.

The Servant, on his appointment, will find himself very busy. None the less, time must be made for those who helped him achieve his position, even if they personally oppose the Prince. It is only by continuing goodwill from all sides that the Servant will be useful to the Prince. In his promotion, the Servant must be careful to take no action that could destroy his myth; he must continue to appear to be the same man.

Machiavelli instructs us that men ought either to be well treated or crushed, because they can avenge themselves of lighter injuries, but not of more serious ones. A good Servant will reflect carefully on this advice and then ignore it, for the Servant's power, although wide ranging, is to deflect, not to destroy. A Servant persuades. Ideally, he never needs to demonstrate his power. The Servant encourages the promotion of his enemies, allowing the promotion to cause their destruction. If by some chance they avoid destruction, their promotion will have removed them from the path that the Servant intends to follow. No man with Machiavelli's philosophy can be employed by a Prince for anything other than carrying out assassinations, after which he must himself be removed.

A Servant must organize his affairs so that there is time to travel throughout the land, and consolidate distant friendships. People in faraway provinces may have power far in excess of their seeming importance. Often they feel neglected. It is not enough to bring them to the capital. By visiting them in their own lands, their greatness is exhibited to friends and acquaintances in their home towns. Never underestimate their pride or their conceit. Men in the regions are always jealous of colleagues from the capital.

There are certain jobs over which the Servant will have an element of direct control. Since it is not wise to fill them with acquaintances, friends, relatives, or strangers, the choice is very difficult. The best-equipped people for these jobs are people who have retired, but they are seldom acceptable, often being said to be too old. So the Servant is forced to choose between the four categories. First he should appoint his relatives. Although these can be as treacherous as anyone else, in the last resort there are other pressures that can keep them under control. If there are no relatives available, the Servant should make the appointments on merit. Never give jobs to friends: they make the most dangerous enemies. Strangers can be useful, and the fact that a man is unknown to the Servant can be a positive advantage, for he can introduce him to new contacts.

The Servant must beware when the Prince wishes to appoint his own relatives. Tread like a cat where the Prince's relatives are concerned. Genius does not run in the blood. Servant, always remember that a Prince will value blood above all, whether he be elected or hereditary. This is part of him; it involves his virility and his conceit. You are dealing with a living manifestation of the Prince's humanity, of his pride. Have as little to do with his heirs as possible. They may have influence with the Prince, but to use them as tools is too risky. Smile at them, bow to them, never criticize when they have committed a folly. Although his fury is originally directed at his child, the Prince may, with time, redirect it at the Servant. The wise Servant will have nothing to do with the relatives of the Prince.

The Servant's public posture must always be against change.

It is in all this that the Servant finds his myth most useful. Always appear to support the old order, and be seen to be conventional. The Servant must never redecorate his office on coming to power; never even rearrange the furniture; no new carpets, no new pictures. He must wear the image of his own predecessor like a glove, but he must also remember that it is his hand inside the glove. The Idea must be radical, but its implementation must be carried out as if no small thing will change. When changes are suggested, never oppose them, but never support them vigorously. The Servant's private position is to support only those reforms demanded by the Idea and necessary to strengthen the Prince's position. The Servant must discover unseen ways to pour adrenalin into the bloodstream of bureaucracy. The reputation of a rival can be damaged by remarks such as, 'He is a fine man, he believes so strongly in change.'

The Prince may wish to introduce reforms for no better reason than a feeling of confidence. The Servant must beware of this: it is the big dipper of fame. Reforms must be undertaken if the Idea requires them. Be very careful of your involvement in the Prince's desire for extra reforms. None the less, the Servant must carry out his will, and it is inevitable that he will make enemies in doing so. Note their names and watch them always. The Idea of the Prince will require the institution of reforms; once these have been carried out, the success of the nation makes further reform unnecessary. The Servant when faced with the danger of casual reform must assess the profit and loss after the Prince has decided on his course, and cause this balance to be shown to the Prince. He must not persuade him to change his mind. Of course, the Servant must, under no circumstances, try to frustrate the Prince: the Idea is the Prince's Idea. If the Idea calls for reform, then there must be reform – in this area it is the Idea that is paramount; it is not the job of the Servant to inhibit the Prince. If the evolution of the Idea needs to be speeded up, the change in it coming suddenly, then this must happen. The Servant can only warn the Prince of what many believe to be the consequences of these actions.

The Servant must be liberal with hospitality; he must show a generous spirit but have a reputation for shrewdness with money. It helps to come from Scotland since people assume this of those who come from that country – and people like nothing more than to believe their prejudices. The Servant must nurture this part of the myth. An ability to raise funds for the benefit of the Prince is of the utmost importance. In the matter of raising money, his ability can be measured exactly by the Prince; no myth can save the Servant here. While cultivating this reputation for generosity, a Servant must be careful not to stray into magnificence. Princes can be critical of the lifestyle of their Servants.

The Servant must be careful with his own funds, for if he were to waste them, he might be driven to dishonesty, or, almost as base, be accused of it. Such an accusation would involve him in a battle which would be a waste of his time, would make the Prince suspicious, and might even bring them both down. The Servant must live within his means, drawing satisfaction only from his work. The Servant must live with style, but this can be done without ever competing with the men of substance. (Note that they will tend to hide their wealth when the Servant comes visiting, lest he should ask them to support the Prince more generously than they have already done.) The Servant must reward smaller supporters out of proportion to their worth. This will make a large impression on them, and they will tell of the Servant's generosity, while richer men talk only of their own. The Servant must take care to see that small men who work for the Prince are well rewarded. The Servant must never be seen to waste the funds of either the Prince or his subjects. Important people are irrelevant in this context, for they are paid in a different coin of far greater value. The Servant may spend small sums from the Prince's funds to reward originality, using these grants to encourage certain groups favourable to the Prince. These funds can become a source of envy, and many people like to have the patronage involved in their distribution. But funds are for winning support, not for the self-promotion of other individuals, and it is the job of the Servant to see that they are used this way.

The Servant understands the social uses of wealth, knowing how to give small amounts to charities, and how, by spending this money, to set up a social web. The Servant knows his wealth is one of his credentials, for people will categorize him immediately if he has money, and this will be to his advantage.

Money can be used wisely, or offensively. The Servant must never believe that because an individual may be offended at receiving money he cannot be bought. The Servant must deal in people, buying and selling them at their own price and in their own currency. It is from having money that some men draw their status, but money alone only gives them power over weaker men. Other men use money to give them true freedom: the ability to choose. The Servant would be wrong to assume, however, that a man who has money has no other talent, for the reverse is likely to be true. The Servant's talent is to understand the employment of funds so that the effect they have will multiply. Should one of these successful men learn the Servant's trade, he could be extremely formidable. Certain individuals feel a need to know people who have money. Others need to reject money, while still using it. Money can be used by the Servant crudely, to buy things, but mostly he deals in persuading people to do things for the

Prince, so the Servant must know how to use money to influence them. The Servant must understand the power of money in other people's eyes. To them money is like a standard that they carry before them. The Servant has no use for money personally; it is only because others believe that money has some real value that the Servant can use it as a means of influence.

The Servant should not acquire property. Having done so he will be disliked by his tenants and his colleagues. Property is too obvious a sign of wealth. It is the same with companies. Having bought them, to make them work he will sometimes have to take stern measures, and consequently will be disliked. Why should the Servant involve himself in these areas of risk? The investments of the Servant must be secret and small in volume. Small investments in a variety of undertakings, placed to give the Servant patronage, are a cheap and very effective way to be popular.

Should the Prince find himself in the wilderness, he will probably be poor. It is the job of the Servant to see to his needs. The Prince, unless he is to retire (when it is best if he too goes to the country and takes up agriculture), must always beware of action that would prejudice his return to power. The Prince must under no circumstances engage in commerce: it is not that the Prince might involve himself in any transaction that would mean that blame could at a later date be attached to him, but that the Prince, being unfamiliar with commerce, might innocently involve himself with those who would undertake such transactions. Those who are Princes, those who will be Princes, and those who have been Princes, must avoid commerce. The raising of money must be left entirely to the Servant, who can be sacrificed in the event of trouble.

When a Prince is in the wilderness, the systems of the State that supported him before will be gone; it is the job of the Servant to see that these are replaced, and that these replacements are independent of vested interests. There are those who, wishing the Prince well, will say, 'Come, join my empire. I will provide for you.' This is not acceptable, for the Prince is a true Prince, not the client Prince of anyone. The Prince must always conduct himself in a way that leaves open the possibility of a return to power. The period in the wilderness must be blameless. The Prince must spend all his time furthering the Idea. The Prince must have the time, the place and the funds to regenerate the Idea, for his enemies will try to destroy the Idea while the Prince is out of power, believing wrongly that in this way they can destroy the Prince. The Servant must gather round the Prince people who supported the Idea. These must be people of intellect whose minds can help the Idea and whose voices can promote it. The Servant must see that the Prince does not waste time on useless undertakings, that he spends no time with those who would waste his time, for in this period when the Prince does not govern he has no need to talk to those who are not his trusted supporters. The Prince must spend all his time preparing the Idea and himself for the future. The Servant has nothing to do with the Idea: he spends all his time in seeing to the needs of the Prince. Among these needs is the promotion of the Prince's own myth. The Servant must travel, tell all of the greatness, the kindness and other attributes of the Prince. The Servant must tell these things in such a way that his hearers will repeat them; the Servant must spend time building the myth of the Prince (for the Prince in the wilderness has need of a myth). The Servant also builds his own myth; the very act of creating a myth is a very important lesson in deception. When telling these things he may use humour, for he needs to be sure that his sayings are repeated.

[48]

A Servant will, as he creates his myth, use a variety of images. As opposed to the myth, which comprises that which is reported of the Servant, an image is what is actually seen or heard of the Servant. The Servant will not manufacture an image whole and new, but will use a series of images that exist already and combine them so they become uniquely his – for instance, by continually smoking cigars, always the same size and always the same make; by attending the opera regularly and always occupying the same seat; by using the same restaurant, always sitting at the same table; by attending the same night club on regular occasions between the same hours. The use of shorthand in creating an image will help the Servant – for example, even though the Servant will be a member of many clubs, he wears always the same club tie, since people will be aware of the significance of the club, its members, and the type of person likely to be a member. The Servant will attend the football matches of a favourite team, go to the horse races, always wear similar suits and shoes. In this way, the Servant can always be found by those who would seek him out, and recognized by those who do not know him. He will seem to be predictable, a quality people find reassuring.

Each of the images the Servant adopts will signal a particular reaction in other people. The Servant must choose each of these images with great care, for they will influence the public view of his character. The Servant must exhibit these images regularly, so that the public identify these images with him, and only him. To change an image will worry the public, and must usually be avoided. The Servant modifies his appearance only to signal a change in his own attitude to events. Using his carefully constructed collection of images as part of the myth which is his shield and disguise, the Servant may still manoeuvre outside his myth and these images, though this must be done secretly. The Servant must be known to always be at certain places at certain times, so that other men may be able to meet him there should they wish to tell him something. They will know that they meet there on purpose, but will believe the Servant to be unaware of this. The Servant must also be aware that, having created the belief that he will regularly attend certain places, should he fail to attend, people will place greater emphasis on the Servant's absence than may be justified. So the Servant, having created an image, must stick to it. This is why he must never take up an image lightly. Creating images can be exciting and entertaining in itself. A man of imagination will find toying with images a seductive alternative to the boredom of an orderly life. The Servant must never fall into the trap of using an image to impress friends (male or female, particularly not female), colleagues or the public. The image must always be complementary and part of the Servant's myth. The image is to be used only to serve the Idea and the Prince.

The Servant must learn not to believe his own publicity. He must also see that the Prince does not believe it either. It is better if the Prince does not read newspapers, for they only say what the Prince's friends wish him to hear or what the Prince's enemies wish the population to believe. They are not suitable evidence to make decisions on; the Prince, being well served, will be informed of events that occur.

Timing is crucial, and must be carefully studied. When something objectionable has to be done, the Servant will want as little public reaction as possible. He needs to study the logistics of the media. The Servant needs to choose a day when there is plenty of other news, for it is better that the Servant's bad news competes for a place to be reported. He may even find it convenient to create other news at that time, as a diversion. The Servant must also consider the time of year; he may choose a time when many people are away. Also he should never tell a writer anything except to influence him. He must be discreet but appear free with information. If you wish a fact to be repeated, make it interesting or humorous. If you wish that fact to remain hidden when questioned about it, make it sound extremely boring. If these rules are followed carefully, it should be possible for the Servant to take objectionable action without too much trouble. The Servant then uses the myth to cover his tracks. The Servant is known by his myth, and it is by his myth that men will judge him. They might say, 'He could not have done such and such; he tells me all that he does, and he said nothing of this.' Or, 'That is totally out of character – the Servant could not have done that.' Even, 'The Servant travels each summer; he was not here.' 'He has no interest in that subject; why would he do that?'

The publication of books must only be for a purpose. Most people do not understand what they read; they glance at the words, then form opinions. The Prince takes a great risk in writing books. A Prince's political memoirs, or even biographies of him, give opponents the opportunity to comment on his performance. Most people read book reviews rather than the books themselves, and since reviews are often written by people hostile to the Prince, these can be very damaging. They can give the impression of opinion forming against the Prince.

The Servant never accompanies the Prince to the theatre, lest he laugh in the wrong place and the Prince misunderstand his attitude, for the Servant, while not agreeing with the playwright, may still find a satirical reference very funny. Princes do not find being mocked at all funny.

Incidentally, the Servant should never forget the power of the political cartoonists. They should be cultivated by the

Servant, and he should occasionally be pictured in their work, for to be occasionally an object of fun is useful to the Servant. It will cause those around the Prince to see him as a less serious figure. The Servant should cause the work of the cartoonists who feature the Prince in a kindly light to be bought, thus encouraging them to continue to do so. Humour is the polish that gives a shine to the Servant's myth. Remember, though, that there is no force so terrible in politics as humour. Never, in jest, say anything that may when repeated interfere with the myth, although jesting is a way of building a myth, for men love to repeat jokes. The use of humour is not to be overlooked, but it must be used very carefully. It is, for example, useful in the destruction of an enemy. Never use a joke unless you intend to.

It is sometimes sensible to try to alter the course of a disaster by trying to turn it into a farce, although only as a last resort. Normally humour is far too unreliable, but it can be used to tell of events without seeming to do so. Humour can be a destroyer, too, but only after careful consideration. Casual jokes must never be used. The funnier the joke, the greater its currency. But, in the course of time, the victim will hear the joke and never forgive the Servant, becoming a dangerous and unnecessary enemy.

Humour can be used by writers to reveal a deeper and unspoken truth, but never, ever, make jokes about a victim. Humour and jokes are not at all the same thing. Enemies can be destroyed slowly with humour. Humour is a slow-acting poison; with time a man can be made to look foolish and of no ability. The joke is the axe, quick and effective. To ridicule another man with a joke is to invite lasting enmity; to be humorous about yourself is to invite affection.

To think in politics is dangerous. To react is less trouble, but unsatisfactory. What has happened has happened. To be instinctive is a problem because it involves the future. To think about the past or the future can endanger the Idea. The Idea must be the touchstone, the guide in all situations.

The Servant ought to beware of men of intellect. They deal in theory. The Servant deals in reality. However much he may be attracted by theory, it is reality that will shape events; he starts with situations not as they were years ago, or will be centuries in the future, but as they are on this day. Then he can arrange the public's perception of them to suit his purpose. This does not mean that the Servant should not mix with intellectuals. Quite the reverse: he must meet and debate with them as often as possible to sharpen his mind, for without constant debate minds quickly go blunt.

I have advised against plotting. Now I will go further. Never plot with the Prince; never tell him of cunning plans to overthrow those who rule in other countries. He must think of these schemes himself. In any court there are people who will urge the ruler to strike down some other ruler, but he must never think of the Servant as a plotter. When the Prince has decided to plot, show him only that you can carry out his wishes efficiently. Fewer men can carry out plots than can concoct them. There is a vital rule to the execution of a plot: credit for it must never be attributed to the Prince or to his Servant, especially if the plot succeeds.

In failure, the Servant has to be quick on his feet. A measure of confusion is the best tactic: total confusion even better. The Servant's myth can be called upon to spread uncertainty. At the worst, the Servant must take the blame. As for success, it is always easy to find someone to take the credit, for the desire to succeed, and to be seen to succeed, is among the greatest of human failings. The Servant's successes must be secret. Every public success makes the next task harder. For example, he may have cultivated a particular high official; this official should not be encouraged to greet the Servant with a kiss, while merely waving at others. This will enrage rivals and they will identify in their jealousy a plot, or see a plan where there is none. There is no sensation so infectious to an alert observer as the current that passes between two men who share a plot. Never forget that the Servant moves in a world of alert observers.

The Servant must never be seen to execute a plot. It is his job to convey the sorrow of the Prince to victims of the plot, to lay the blame broadly, and to offer help in their adversity to those who have been overthrown. The Servant must spread stories of the Prince's generosity, for the wise Prince never claims victories as a result of a plot. It has succeeded if his enemies discover that their plans have been set back. The Servant views the outcome with the appearance of sadness, especially if an idle courtier takes credit for the plot himself. As for the victim of a plot, he must be found an occupation quickly where his new colleagues will be keen that he does not bring them all into disrepute by speaking ill of the Prince.

The Servant will dine with the Prince from time to time and when he does so, he should never raise serious matters. He should be humorous at meals, he should have a light touch with the Prince, using humour, not making jokes. The Servant must ensure that the Prince knows that he will never press him with difficult questions, for the Prince knows well that these difficult questions have to be answered, and he will not care to have to give that answer as he eats. The Prince will not invite a man to dine with him often who disrupts the Prince's dining. It is possible that the Prince may raise a serious matter; only then does the Servant speak seriously. The reasons for dining with the Prince are fourfold: first, always to be available to be asked any serious question; the second, to collect the trivia about the court and the Prince; third, to let others know that he dines with the Prince; and fourth, to listen to what those others who dine with the Prince have to say.

The Servant must never try to advise the Prince who he should or should not see: influence should only be brought to bear on which people get to see the Prince. It is the power of access that is the real power: it is difficult to influence a Prince you cannot see, or see at the wrong moment. By far the best form of access is when the Prince travels. The Servant should always travel with people he wishes to lobby.

In politics, access is the most vital factor. However much people plot and plan, they can be brought to nothing by access. It is important that the Servant identifies and gets to know all the minor officials in the departments of the grand officials with whom he has dealings. For instance, the office of the Prince may be controlled by a relatively minor official or chief-of-staff. While the chief-of-staff must never appreciate that he personally is not being cultivated, do not waste any time on this man. Real power is in the hands of the keeper of the diary.

Access can be used in two ways: either to allow a man to put a plan to the Prince, or to stop him from doing so. This process is conducted not by forbidding the man to see the Prince, rather by arranging appointments at a time when the Prince is either too busy or has spare time, depending on the desired result. It is foolish to bring a complicated issue to a Prince in a hurry. This makes it unnecessary ever to forbid appointments to people anxious to see the Prince.

Access can be used to destroy or advance; for advancement

it is clearly necessary to choose the right time for the man who is to be advanced to see the Prince. And the right mood. Not so much the mood of the Prince: rather, it is important for the Servant to get the man he wishes to advance into the right mood to impress the Prince. But the Servant can also destroy a man by arranging access at the wrong time. The time when the Prince has other matters on his mind or is in a hurry to leave for an appointment to which he has been looking forward, this is a particularly deadly time, for the Prince will be in a good humour when he greets his visitor, and this visitor with his time-wasting rubbish will spoil a day that the Prince thought he was going to enjoy, so it is unlikely that the Prince will be keen to see this visitor again. This is a certain way to ensure that the Prince is not impressed with the man. Or maybe the Servant can wait until the Prince is deep in conversation, and then suggest that this person should interrupt, telling him that the Prince is keen to have his views on foreign policy, or the rating system. This has an additional advantage because the victim is left with the impression that the Servant has done him a favour.

A man who argues intelligently is hard to deal with in this way. The Servant must have prepared the Prince to receive such a man, giving the Prince information to construct arguments to counter those of the intelligent man. He may not be an enemy of the Servant or Prince; his arguments may turn out to be extremely helpful, or if not he must be destroyed by promotion. But he must not, under any circumstances, be ignored by the Prince or frustrated by the Servant.

Another use of access to destroy is to invite a man to put a plan to the Prince when the Servant knows in advance that he will disapprove. This will damage the man in the Prince's estimation. The danger of access is that people will often say more than they intended, and so set off unpredictable trains of thought in the Prince. The Servant must judge carefully the amount of time that a man needs to deliver his message: short messages need only a short space of time, and even if the messenger is a friend of the Servant he must be allowed only a few minutes. He must not be allowed time to spoil a good case. If he is a friend of the Prince this is even more important. The Servant must be alert to this risk and be skilled in bringing an interview to an end. The Servant must also ensure that there is time for himself to meet with the Prince, for Princes can often become overwhelmed by the affairs of state, seeing only representatives of other nations, leaving little time for their own Servants.

In this matter of meetings, the Servant must be a master mechanic. In meetings he keeps silent. What needs to be done must have been dealt with before the meeting begins. Most of the statements made at meetings are repetitive, people saying the same things in different ways, each one trying to take the credit for the original statement.

If the Servant has arranged things well, someone else will always say what he has in mind, and he can remain silent as long as his aims are being achieved, for the Servant goes to a meeting to achieve an end, not to demonstrate his cleverness. Sometimes, a meeting will begin to go off course, and then the Servant will have to speak. First he picks on an inaccuracy made by some minor figure. By savaging him, he ensures that he is listened to at meetings.

The Servant chooses the minor figure because it is easier to win the argument. More important, as the Servant will have to make his peace with him later, this minor figure may very well come to hold the Servant in high regard: the minor figure will be content with a small benefice or even a few kind words. Major figures do not like to be savaged in front

[57]

of their colleagues – it might well cost the Servant much to repair the damage. In argument, should it eventually become necessary, the Servant should start by agreeing with people's beliefs, only gradually changing his view from theirs to his, at the same time carrying them with him. The Servant never argues for pleasure.

It is virtually impossible to implement any action in anything like its original form after a lengthy debate. There will always be compromisers, and, given the nature of any debate, they are likely to win. This is particularly true of a public debate, where these compromisers can pose as moderates, when in reality they are men without any very firm commitment. If something objectionable must be done, it should be done without the benefit of debate.

The Servant must never allow secret meetings to take place in his home, or any other property he may own. The risk is that the outcome of secret meetings will draw attention to him. These meetings will always be tagged with the name of the place where they were held. This will always be an embarrassment to the Servant, since it always brings his home to the mind of the Prince whenever a disastrous meeting is recalled, especially as the Servant's enemies will take care to mention it.

It is the job of the Servant, however, to provide places for these meetings and he can, if these meetings are successful, always choose a name for them that will be to his advantage. There are many men who would seek a place in history. Name a meeting after one of them. They will readily lend a house and pay for the privilege of doing the Servant favours. It is strange, this desire of men to be remembered. Name a dish by a famous chef after one of your guests, let him see it on the menu in a popular restaurant – you cannot imagine the man's delight.

The Servant must be skilled in the use of language. For example, he will leave a word hanging. He rehearses this, carefully choosing the word that he will throw into the conversation. The idea is to nudge the talk in the right direction. Do not spell things out. The politician will use a phrase repeatedly; he will take three arguments and discard two, repeating the third three times, for the audience does not hear it at once, and the second time does not properly understand. The politician works with repetition and emphasis. The Servant, who is not a politician and must never imagine that he is, works not through repetition, but through suggestion, and he uses only the subtlest forms of suggestion. Now it might be said that this technique could never penetrate the barrage of words that comes from politicians. This is why the ground must be carefully prepared, so that when politicians do hear a suggestion they will seize it for their own, repeating it endlessly.

The Servant must be adept at the drafting of documents, for he will appreciate the power of words. By his choice of words, he is able to persuade, which is a far more powerful weapon than force. The Servant must often practise this. When he starts to persuade, the Servant will use the same technique as when he argues. He will agree with his opponent and slowly change his opponent's view, moving gradually from position to position, always agreeing with him, and displaying a detachment from the Servant's own stated views. Sometimes, the Servant will even criticize his own opinions, but always he draws the views of his opponent closer to his own – until the opponent discovers that he is, after all, an ally of the Servant, and will do his bidding.

[59]

It is worth noting that the agreements reached at most meetings are based on a mutual misunderstanding of those agreements but, as time will pass before they are implemented, this does not matter. By then one side or the other will have become the more powerful, and their views will prevail. Moreover, many of the clauses people wish to have in documents are of no account, for they are there to cover all eventualities; in politics this is not necessary as time moves very quickly. In the art of negotiation, it is important to give way quickly on a few small items. The Servant will agree to anything, provided he knows it cannot happen, and he will always be prepared to retreat from his views and agree with an opponent provided he is confident that he is able to reverse the result of that agreement at a later date.

In argument the Servant usually tries to elevate the tone, only putting people down when it is absolutely necessary, and then only very occasionally. He will make his opponents feels better for losing by taking their reasoning, extending it until it appears ridiculous, and then laughing before admitting that he is wrong. The Servant tries never to ridicule and cause one man to laugh at another. He laughs only at himself. Nobody who negotiates with the Servant must feel bitterness. In argument he will use pathos, in such a way that the opponent does not know whether to laugh or to cry. Then the Servant will play on his opponent's emotions in the least expected way. Here words must be chosen with care. The Servant fits the words to the situation, using a short word if there is only time for a short word. Timing is of vital importance to the argument. Use a long word as you would use a pause, and use a long word for effect, but never too many. When the Servant wishes the opponent to speak, he will fall silent, for men find it hard not to fill a silence with their words. If the Servant remains silent for long enough, the opponent will say something he had no intention of saying.

This is a case of leaving silences for fools to talk into. The Servant never uses words the opponent cannot understand. He avoids this apparent advantage, for in reality it makes his opponent feel inadequate, and therefore wary. The Servant must also be careful of bringing new facts into the argument, since their impact can be unpredictable. He argues along the lines that he has planned.

The Servant must be skilled in interpreting documents. He must fully understand the meaning of words and also appreciate that words do not always mean what they were intended to mean. The Servant must also be skilled in adjusting the meaning of words and follow the advice of Humpty Dumpty: 'Words mean what I wish them to mean and, if I use them often, I pay them overtime.' (The Servant never hesitates to borrow a phrase from a man of greater talent.)

The Servant must know men who understand words and men who understand policy. These will be different men, for they are different trades. The Servant must also know men who are skilled in the selling of words once they have been written, for this is yet another trade. The Servant must be certain that each of these skilled operators practise only their own trade for, inevitably, each of them will long to practise the other's. When words are written by them, they must be the Prince's words, reflecting the Idea in every respect.

The Servant must see that the Prince is not swayed in this matter by clever words for, in the world of politics, if an action seems to be clever, or if it is to be taken because it is convenient, it is likely to be wrong. Politics is about simplicity and the future, and the real art of politics is about surviving long enough to implement the Idea. For the Prince and the Servant and the Idea, short-term gain is of no advantage. It is of no interest to them just to govern. The ground must be prepared to receive the Idea, for they are interested in governing only according to the Idea; merely occupying a job has no appeal to them. The Prince and the Servant will use images, the myth and any other means to achieve this.

The messenger of a Prince is a man of great power. A messenger bearing a message to the Prince is in great danger. Who knows how it will be received? Never be the bearer of bad news. The Servant has to see that the Prince's messages are delivered as they were intended. It is easy for a messenger to deliver the same words in many different ways so that, for example, angry words seem soft to the recipient. The messenger will always be tempted to alter the emphasis of words to deter wrath or to increase his own prestige. The words of the Prince must be delivered as they were sent. There must be no misunderstanding. Use no more words than are necessary to make their meaning known.

It is better that the messenger is unfamiliar with the events that surround a message, since he is less likely to place his own interpretation on it. Never let men deliver a message who have been involved in the policy in question, or men who could benefit or, worst of all, forget a part of it. The best messengers are distant from the Prince, but known to the Servant.

Monuments must always be large and preferably very ugly. They should be built to commemorate past regimes; people will recognize their ugliness and resent them. Always promote past regimes; show them to be powerful, for this enhances the prestige of the Prince, since they are gone and he rules. Accord them plenty of glory, for there is no harm in this. Beware of shrines, such as a spot on the pavement where people commemorate a potent cause with flowers. These shrines are extremely dangerous, especially when they are in open spaces where people can gather. Praise the cause, and gain the sympathy of the people. Agree that flowers should be laid, but say that there is a need for a greater monument on this spot; replace the simple shrine with a very large complex for public use, named after the cause of the shrine. Fill the space so that people no longer meet there. Build extravagance where there once was simplicity and the cause of the shrine will lose support. The sponsors of the shrine will find it hard to oppose the generosity of the Prince, both in terms of money and his attitude to the enemy. The people, really preferring a useful building to a shrine, will support the Prince.

The Servant should persuade the Prince to erect many statues, particularly to the heroes of his opponents. These should be erected where they interrupt the flow of traffic, or cut off a favourite pedestrian path, so that the public will react against them. In time they can be pulled down with public approval. The building of such statues is how the Servant deals with the image of the Prince's opponents: he promotes them to a position that is ludicrous.

While learning his trade, the Servant must travel. By visiting other cities he learns the feel of greatness, and begins to understand the use of monuments, for they are the impedimenta of history. Furthermore, the Prince may call on him to deliver messages to foreign rulers and it is as well to know the people to whom they are to be delivered, for it may be that the Prince needs the help of foreign friends to support and promote him. It is also useful for the Servant to be in a position to recommend the Prince's messenger to them. The assistants of these friends must be known to the Prince's Servant. It is always important for the Servant to make contacts with men before they rise to fame. Many will achieve nothing, but those who do will know the Servant is not interested in them only because of their fame. (The Servant must never stress the fact that he knew them before they were famous since they may not recognize a time when they were unknown.)

I have used the word 'man' in the old-fashioned sense, but not through any belief that only men are capable of operating in the world of Princes. Indeed, there are many women who play quite as significant a role as men. I use 'man' simply because I dislike the words that have been invented to cover both sexes at their work. So calling all those in active politics 'men', I would now like to refer to those involved on the periphery as 'women', for that is mainly what they are. The Servant must be friendly with many of these women, entertaining them often, taking trouble to win their goodwill.

The Servant would do well to operate through these women, using them to gather and pass information. It is important that they are never given the feeling that they are being used. Rather, they should always feel that they are being useful. The desire to be useful is very strong; the pleasure at being included in a secret is very great; the urge to be party to a seeming plot is irresistible. The Servant will find no shortage of women to help him, and many men will listen to these women, and, out of conceit, will tell them many things which they, from excitement, will repeat to the Servant.

The advantage of these women is that while they are outside politics and affairs of state, they meet regularly with others who are greatly involved in both. These people can be very useful to the Servant for delivering his messages, apparently impartially, or indeed unawares. They are good at passing information for they love to talk, although they often do not know the significance of what they say. Conversely, the

Servant must always beware of women who may be used as traps by his enemies.

The Servant appreciates the need for care in the matter of sex. He will listen to women and pay much attention to what they say, for this is what they enjoy most. When listening, the Servant is not telling, and by not telling, remains secure. Many of the great Servants have worked through women, for they attend parties and have time to move around society and politics and in and out of houses where they hear a great deal. One of the great Servants in recent times, by chance a woman, employed men for this purpose, but men are often suspicious of other men. Women will not suspect the Servant, particularly if he listens carefully to their talk.

As for sex, the Servant must have none of it, never lusting after the women of others. This excites jealousy and all sorts of other, less predictable, adventures. Never pursue women. Apart from anything else, men will boast about the pursuit and this is a great danger, both because of the indiscretion itself, and because boasting is a habit more easily acquired than lost. Being a man of supreme imagination, the Servant will meet a better class of woman in his dreams, and these women come when the mind calls and go at its command, silently, telling nothing.

As I have said, the Servant sacrifices all for the Prince and the Idea. He must give up all his own ideas to concentrate on his task, but it is vital that the Servant moves in society. He must attend the opera, parties, everywhere that people gather, for he must always be listening for information and spreading goodwill for the Prince. The way that these people view the Servant is very important. The Servant must have a working knowledge of the arts, literature and sport, for he must seem at home at these gatherings. He must never claim great knowledge of these subjects, only an interest in them. If he claims knowledge that he does not possess in these matters he will easily be found out and so allow himself to become despised, which would greatly damage his value to the Prince. He must be discreet, giving just enough information to make his company sought after. He will always say that he knows no secrets because people will believe the opposite. This is as it should be, because the Servant must never leave the impression that he is kept in ignorance on any matter. If there is a subject about which discretion does not allow him to reveal even one small piece of news, it should not be discussed at all; for in revealing small pieces of news to an alert listener he risks revealing all. It can be perilous for the Servant to mislead people; they do not like it and they will grow to mistrust him. The Servant's myth must be that of an honest and interesting person. He should never imagine that he will make friends by telling secrets. The Servant must say nothing in confidence. Confidence does not exist.

The Servant must suggest to the Prince that he entertains, and let everyone know how much the Prince likes to entertain. The Servant must be responsible for these entertainments and will see that, though the banquets are large, for many people must be entertained and none must be left out, they are none the less modest. The Servant will use this as evidence of the Prince's generosity and his modesty. The choice of food and drink at these entertainments is a matter of careful judgement. The Servant himself also entertains, but on a much smaller scale, and in an intimate manner. He serves only the best food and drink, for these will attract people to his table from whom he can learn much and who he can, in turn, influence. There are few people so important that they will turn down an invitation to dine where the host employs a great chef. The Servant must employ the greatest chef and maintain a brilliant wine cellar. It is very important that he is known for both these things.

At functions attended by the Prince, the Servant should, when appropriate, be there as well, watching from a distance to see if he can be of help. The Servant must not engage the Prince in conversation. The object is for the Prince to meet other people, not to take up his time talking to the Servant, which only causes envy and annoyance to the others at the function. The Servant must ensure that he is seen once by the Prince. This is called 'being seen by the widow', after the practice at Jewish funerals. The Servant may be tempted to introduce someone to the Prince whom he feels he ought to meet. He must resist the temptation. The ground must be carefully prepared for all introductions, and an introduction to a Prince is too serious a business to be risked at a party. Many men at parties will try to meet the Prince. Those whom the Servant would introduce must be of use to the Prince and the Idea.

The Servant should have many casual friends who will speak well of him. They will praise him to the Prince in the hope that this will improve their own position, and the Prince will understand the praise for what it is. But some of it will stick, and improve the position of the Servant. But he should never rely on his friends. His only deep relationship is with the Prince and the Idea.

Machiavelli is of the opinion that Princes should be protected from flatterers. This is wrong. Flattery will stimulate the Prince and is better for him than alcohol. Princes need flattery to encourage them, on occasions to raise their spirits, and as long as they truly know the nature of flattery (and the Prince will certainly know that) there is no harm in it. The Servant should beware those men whose honest intention is to tell the Prince 'the truth', for they repeat only their own opinions or their own view of events, and such opinions are worth only as much as the men who give them. Indeed, these opinions are worth less than those who offer them, if that is possible. Although these men may be sincere, their opinions will be coloured by their own interests. The Prince, on the other hand, has to make a decision in his interest and in the interest of the Idea, and his judgement must not be coloured by the likes and dislikes, anger, fear and greed of others. The Servant should encourage flatterers and discourage those prophets of gloom who are just as likely to be wrong in their judgements as the tellers of truth. Right or wrong, they will depress the Prince. The Servant must beware the reaction of the Prince to these prophets of doom: the desire to avoid all men and all advice and, in time, all news.

An able flatterer is a useful man at court, for if he is good at his job, he will be seen for what he is and no danger will come of it. The flattery of enemies must be examined with great attention, for in their flattery they can reveal secrets. The Prince should listen to these enemies, but must not be deceived by their goodwill. When he receives this goodwill, which is a reflection of his own success, he must use it, but it is vital that he does not believe it. Should a policy fail, the Servant will find that his enemies have predicted it. His job is to transform their predictions so they look like support, by recalling selective quotations from their earlier flattery.

At times the Prince may need to be reassured, may truly need flattery, and then it is the job of the Servant to see that he gets it. It will do no harm for, as I have said, flattery will not alter the judgement of the Prince. The Prince must see many people and hear all manner of things. Princes do not need to be told of their mistakes. There is nothing more annoying than to be told that you are wrong when you know it already.

[68]

It is important that the Prince enjoys flattery and fully understands its value. A Servant must ensure that the Prince has time to listen to other men; this will flatter them. There are many reasons why the Prince will listen, and few of them are for enlightenment. Only a bad Prince tries to be the same as his followers. Men like to be led by a Prince. Indeed, many men want to be Princes themselves. Men will not want to be with a Prince who spends his whole time doing as others wish. If he wishes to flatter, the Prince must listen to these men, who will tell him he is a Prince, and then how he should behave. The Prince will know that they can never be the Prince themselves.

About these people who press their company on the Prince: never warn him against them individually. Rely on technicalities and the jealousy of colleagues to see that their views do not prosper. The Prince, like most humans, can tire of fellow human beings, and the Servant must watch for this, constantly placing the person he wishes to destroy in the path of the Prince until the Prince begins to ask what he is doing there. At that point the Servant may, just by chance, fail to find a convincing explanation of that man's role.

Machiavelli says that by acquiring the love of the population, the Prince will prevent them plotting against him. But it is not the population that does the plotting. Plots are hatched by senior officials and colleagues of the Prince. Plots are seldom hatched successfully by his avowed enemies. The views of the population only provide the ammunition for these plots, and these views are only what clever plotters would have them be. Plotters will say 'the people believe this, or believe that', but the people are mostly unaware that their desires are being used to further a plot. Those who claim to express the desires of the people are reluctant to ask the people publicly to express themselves. They claim to act on behalf of the people, but they do so with no mandate.

The Servant must take the view that his colleagues will plot against the Prince all the time, even if they do so only in their minds. Grand officials will either agree with the Prince's Idea, in which case they will try to steal it, or they will disagree with the Idea, in which case they will try to destroy it. The Prince must not concern himself with plots or plotters. The population has no interest in plots.

The Prince's enemies and the enemies of the Idea will plot to turn the will of the people against him, and the Servant will counter this not by cunning, but by the strength of the Prince's Idea. The Servant cannot rely on the love of colleagues or the observations of petty officials to warn him of attack, so he must constantly be aware of the meetings of the Prince's colleagues. As plots are secret, plotters will meet privately to avoid discovery by the Servant. The Servant must constantly monitor the places people frequent, and if the Prince's colleagues are not to be found there, he must wonder why. Most plotting is done in the homes of the plotters and therefore remains secret. The Servant must never tell the Prince of these plots, for to tell him would not, in the end, promote the Servant's cause, or further the power of the Idea. The Servant must know of them only to give the correct evidence to the Prince when he has to take action.

Machiavelli gives several examples of complicated plots: of Annibale Bentivogli, for example, who, as Prince of Bologna, was murdered by the Canneschi. He tells how the people then rose and killed the Canneschi, so great was their love of Annibale Bentivogli. It could be that Annibale Bentivogli was murdered by another party, whose aim was to put the blame on the Canneschi. In a democracy, murder is not a practical political tool, but it is realistic to plan to shift the blame, marshalling the anger of the population to destroy an enemy who played no part at all in the plot. It is always hard to get to the bottom of a plot, to find out who really should be blamed. Do not waste time on this exercise. It does not matter. All those involved share the blame in one way or another.

Machiavelli remarks that individuals must never be annoyed but utterly destroyed. Individuals can be destroyed by the device of encouraging them to behave like nobles for, although there is still a certain amount of respect for the nobility, officials, both grand and small, are jealous of newly ennobled figures. The greater the apparent prestige of these people, the less their real influence with the Prince, or, for that matter, anyone else. In order to destroy, promote as high as possible. Promotion to a second chamber is one way. Many men who are prepared to honour the man who has been promoted will resent the thought that his heirs, who deserve no honour, will benefit. Seeing these heirs promoted above them, they will be deeply jealous and work against the recipient of the honour, where before they were indifferent. For those engaged in these affairs lack generosity of spirit. They do not realize how little consequence their spite is to the Prince and the Idea. The Servant must never be spiteful and must never allow himself to deal in actions or thoughts that come from spite.

Having encouraged a man to behave like a noble, a hint to his colleagues that it would not be against the Prince's will if he were destroyed will cause them to tear him apart. This is destruction by elevation, the pulling down of a man by an act of generosity, so achieving the Prince's aim with no blame attaching to the Prince. For the Prince is a generous man who promoted the victim. The blame attaches to the man's rivals,

[71]

jealous men, envious of his promotion. In the destruction of this man they make themselves vulnerable, and so inhibit their capacity to become powerful. At the same time, the myth of the Servant remains one of nobility.

There are certain areas of public life that are small but vital, like the arts. The Servant must see that the Prince, if he is not interested in the arts himself, appoints someone who understands the working of that world, remembering that the arts are a perfect distraction for a political enemy. They could also be a distraction for the Prince whose job it is to implement an Idea – he should waste no time on them, using them only occasionally for personal pleasure. The political enemy will be occupied fully, for the politics of the arts are far more complex and consume much more time than the politics of ruling whole nations. Those who take up these posts in the arts with enthusiasm are instantly lost to the world of plots and treachery, and their silence is cheaply bought; a few pounds for a favourite opera, or the purchase of a picture by the gallery that they command. There is no possibility of a man building a political base from within the world of the arts, and it makes an excellent parking lot for troublesome politicians. It must be arranged that they are in no position to complain without seeming churlish. The Servant must see that all their vanities are satisfied, and must also ensure that the people observe that these vanities have been satisfied. In reality it is impossible to satisfy their vanities, because these men will always call for more.

Those involved in the arts are extremely dangerous, for they form what was once called 'the chattering classes'. These men have to talk, to talk of a past that was never as they describe, to talk of a future that will never be as they hope, and their words are listened to by those who would direct fashion and presume to form the opinions of the people. The

[72]

Servant knows that these men are of little account in the matter of achievement, but he also knows that their words count for much among those of their own class, so he must show them deep friendship (this is part of his myth). Moreover, any success that they may achieve does not make them popular, either with the party or the people at large. He must help them in their continued calling for money to promote their own interests and enthusiasms. By their self-seeking actions those in the arts alienate themselves from the citizens, who by contrast are interested first in finding work and then in entertainment, usually of a sort that these men would have only contempt for.

The Servant must never stress how easy it is to get rid of Servants. The Prince already knows this and will think that the Servant feels insecure and is therefore unreliable, and possibly dangerous. Consequently a shrewd Prince would exclude him from his council, and he would become like any other hired servant, of no use to himself or the Prince, or the Idea.

Princes sometimes like to tell secrets. A good Servant will avoid hearing them, especially any secret that, to be kept, ultimately requires the Servant's death. Knowledge of such a secret will always worry the Prince and he will blame himself for telling this important fact to the Servant in the first place. There is no emotion so destructive of the relationship between the Prince and the Servant as the Prince knowing that he has made a mistake. He may forgive the Servant's mistakes, but not his own, ever. The fact is that this secret will in the end destroy the whole scheme of the Prince, the Servant and the Idea. Do not, under any circumstances, accept a secret from a Prince. Secrets are of very little use to a Servant other than to bolster his pride. The information that the Servant needs is a vast quantity of everyday trivia about the Prince's life. With this information, there is no secret at which the Servant cannot guess. The Prince feels secure because his Servant knows no secrets, and the Servant feels secure because he knows all secrets.

There is but one thing to be remembered: that the secret does not exist, nothing is ultimately secret. Secrets recorded in diaries, however long delayed, will eventually become known. The Servant must proceed in his negotiations on the basis that all will at some time be made public. He can, however, assume some flexibility over the timing of this publicity.

. The man who would do you a favour is your friend for life. The one who would ask a favour will one day be your enemy. The giving of true friendship is the greatest gift that one man can give another, and he that would give this friendship can always be relied upon. The receiving of favours without bitterness needs a man with a character as generous as the one who would do him the favour. The Servant should always beware of those whom he has helped and rely totally on those who have helped him.

The best advice the Servant can have will come from his enemy for he, if he is competent, will have studied the Servant most closely. A great enemy will have taken the trouble to discover all facets of the Servant's character in order to destroy him. The Servant has created his myth to shield his real character from such an enemy. The truly great enemy may penetrate the Servant's myth. As this enemy acts against the Servant, he will reveal to him weaknesses that the Servant did not know existed; these weaknesses have to be quickly repaired. To be attacked by a great enemy is not always bad. In fact, it is part of the training of the Servant for, should he survive this attack, the Servant will be better fitted to serve the

Prince and the Idea. The Servant need not seek out enemies to attack him as the Prince and the Idea prosper; they will appear, and, because of the experience gained, each one is easier to defeat than the one before. But never become complacent because of the ease with which enemies have been dispatched in the good times. Prepare always for bad times, when conflict with even the smallest of enemies could so weaken the Prince that others, seeing this, attack him and win. Always remember that dragons in shallow water are the sport of shrimps. Small men who openly attack the Prince must be defeated publicly and a great spectacle made of it, to encourage the Prince's followers and to discourage enemies. The small enemy must then be made to appear important in some other occupation, by the means that I have described before. Never fight battles for entertainment.

The Servant knows that a war is not won by a simple victory, or lost, for that matter, by a defeat. Rather, his concern is how the Prince will use that victory or defeat. Therefore the Servant must prepare the Prince for either outcome, allowing neither excessive rejoicing nor despair to affect the final outcome of these wars.

The Servant must prepare the Prince for retreat both physically and mentally, so that he has a strong refuge and a firm will to fight again. He also prepares for victory, so that the Prince does not pay too much attention to it, nor waste time on celebrations, which is what many around him will want. The Servant and the Prince must resist celebrating victories, for out of these celebrations comes only jealousy – it is important when this is done that no one should feel left out. The Prince must continue to carry out his Idea as if this conflict had never taken place. Battles are only distractions and, whichever way they go, they must not be allowed to divert him for long. In defeat or victory the Prince still expresses the Idea, and all that will have changed is that he has either more or less power to promote it.

In the case of elected Princes, elections have to be fought as the Prince would fight a war. He is the general responsible for all things: the Prince appoints, the Prince dismisses. In an election no detail should be left to chance; all decisions must be made by the Prince. Others will imagine that these decisions are theirs, and in peacetime this may be so, but in wars and elections the Prince must decide everything. Fame or blame is his. The Servant must not allow men to believe in false victories: to win is to gain ground and to lose is to retreat. To still hold power yet to be forced to retreat is not a victory – it is better for all men to realize this. The Servant must not encourage the celebration of false victories, for men will conclude that they did well when they really need to alter their style of warfare in order to win in the battles that will surely follow. Always beware complacency; the Servant must review the tactics of battle, improving them constantly and treating even true victories as if they were defeats.

The Servant who understands that an effective means of damaging a rival is to promote him, must beware of those who would promote the Servant's own fame. The Servant must never appear to be powerful. His master must always believe that the Servant has no interest in power and that his interest lies only in service. Generosity and strength of character, weaknesses or ruthlessness may be obscured by the Servant's myth, but not power, and any attempt to promote the Servant's fame must be stopped at once. Efficiency and service are the only qualities that the Prince must see in the Servant. The people, if they are aware of him at all, must see him as human. The Servant must see himself as ruthless. There is no action that the Servant will not take to assist the

Prince further the Idea. This sense of purpose is nowhere revealed in the Servant's myth.

The Servant must never be seen to promote the fame of grand figures, for they tend to resent the help of others, however pleased they may appear to be at the time. When these grand figures have their positions improved the Servant will influence these appointments, and if he wishes to assist a colleague, will pass the credit to him. Most people are perfectly happy to take the credit for the promotion of others.

In the case of minor figures who have no other chance for promotion, the Servant must take all credit, even if he had no hand in the matter. This is always possible, because the Servant will have prior knowledge of these appointments. The Servant's myth will be strengthened by his being seen to help these minor figures.

The Servant should occasionally make it his business to reward people who will catch the imagination of the public. To recommend a small medal for a popular entertainer is good for the Prince and costs nothing. It is strange how people love medals, how even those with grand hereditary titles are pleased to wear them. Most men seek rewards that they find hard to achieve, or even rewards that there is no chance of their receiving. This should be encouraged. The Servant must never believe that a man's ambitions have been fulfilled, or that a man is too grand for a flamboyant but small reward.

The Servant should become intimately acquainted with the varieties of revenge. Machiavelli's advice in this matter is good for both the Prince and the Servant: 'When he seizes a state the new ruler ought to determine all the injuries that he will need to inflict. He should inflict them once for all, and not have to renew them every day.' Machiavelli is right: all actions should be taken at once to diminish the power of enemies, but revenge should be used only sparingly, if at all. Revenge should not be used against a fallen enemy; in that case generosity is a more certain weapon. Revenge must be used only by the Prince, and it must be sudden and sure. The Servant's armoury does not contain revenge and his myth contains no hint of revenge. Figures who cross the Servant are cut down by their colleagues. The Servant must always smile goodwill on all. He has no feelings but the feelings of the Prince, and it is only at the bidding of the Prince that these figures find that the tide of life has moved against them. The Servant, like the Prince and the Idea, always moves forward; it is their purpose always to improve; they have no time for, and no interest in, revenge.

I have spoken of how rivals must be dealt with. Now I will discuss how a system of alliances changes after a rival has been removed. Do not assume that because men help the Servant to remove a rival, they do this entirely for his sake. They hope to make a step up for themselves. Today's champion is tomorrow's enemy. The removal of a rival may therefore necessitate the removal of a whole string of rivals, even if this leaves the Servant with a great deal more work to do himself. Consequently, I counsel that the best way of dealing with rivals is to increase the number of their own employees and followers (there are few who can resist the lure of a new assistant), and then to draw this excess to the notice of the Prince. The rival, if he is dismissed, will leave others behind capable of carrying out the work.

Even if he follows these rules, the Servant will always be subject to attack. So let us consider the position of the weakened Servant. Having been driven back, he will have to seek allies. And if he should win, these allies will become his enemies; seeing the Servant remove his enemy, it will occur to them that it may not be hard to remove the Servant. They must be disposed of immediately. This is difficult, and only a Prince can accomplish it. But if the Servant does not get rid of them, they will feed off him. Indeed, this may be the time for the Servant to publicize his victory and then to retire with honour to take up agriculture, for he can win only a certain number of public battles. The number of private battles that he can win is endless. It is often better for the Servant to leave a tiresome rival in his position, and put up with his attacks, than to destroy him and leave a vacuum for some equally tiresome but unknown rival to fill.

Better for the Servant to avoid a fight, but if he is drawn into one, he must be totally unscrupulous, using all his personal knowledge of his opponents to discredit them. He will set the retired men of good repute on his staff to slander his enemies. Although it is out of their character (this makes the slander more effective), they will do so because without the Servant they are nothing, and the Servant, whom they trust, will suggest words for them to say. Those organizations, clubs, and societies that the Servant has assiduously supported must be turned on the enemies of the Servant. They will provide seemingly neutral opinions. The use of neutral opinions in politics is of the highest importance for it has credibility far beyond what it deserves, as men seldom study the source of independent opinions but always believe them.

The Servant lives with danger, and must constantly be aware of attack. This requires him to be an expert in the area where he wishes to fight, for the Servant must always choose his own ground, ground that he has prepared with many traps for his enemies. He can do this by retreating until he reaches it, so the battle will be well within his capacity. The Servant never fights an offensive battle; his offensives are silent offensives. Since he works through influence, nobody is quite sure if he has won or lost until the result becomes obvious. He must also plan for every eventuality. However many the numbers on the dice, the sum of the numbers made by each throw must benefit the Servant in some way or another. But the best defence of all is his myth, which will suggest that he is a harmless figure. Because he is only the Servant, few will waste their time attacking him.

Servants are seldom attacked by the Prince's enemies, but often attacked by those who call themselves the Prince's friends. The Prince's enemies attack only the Prince. The Prince's so-called friends wish to remove the Servant to put a placeman in his job, and so in time bring down the Prince. They are enemies of the Prince, but not worthy of the name of enemies.

I mentioned before how Machiavelli counsels that when a person has to be destroyed, he should be destroyed utterly. This rule should not be applied to organizations, or to the people who run them. Often, when an organization has grown large and exhibits the trappings of power, its idea has in reality grown weak. When the people see a few men enjoying this power and its trappings they find it difficult to believe in the idea, for these men use the organization to improve their lifestyle and are not interested in the idea which originally made the organization powerful. These men are not Princes; these men are not a serious threat, for their idea is in the wilderness, unused, an embarrassment. They must be encouraged in these worthless activities, in the pursuit of greed and self-promotion, for the Servant and the Prince and the Prince's Idea can only benefit from their folly. Now if, as Machiavelli suggests, these men are destroyed, they may well become martyrs, and their idea, freed from their incompetence, will become strong again and may bring down the Prince, the Idea and the Servant too.

So there must be no martyrs. Instead, control of these organizations must be relocated, their very purpose for existence changed, and their leaders rendered harmless. Having become dependent on their trappings, these people can be destroyed by removing their paraphernalia. Do not hand this paraphernalia on to anyone else, because in time these people, or others like them, could restore its potency. For instance, their buildings must be torn down, for if they stay intact, they might become shrines. It is always possible that the empty space where once these buildings stood could become a shrine, so the space must have a popular use. In a busy city it might be transformed into a hospital or multistorey car park; in the country, into a building for growing food, the keeping of large numbers of pigs, perhaps housing for chickens and the intensive production of eggs. As I have said, it is difficult to erect or maintain a shrine on ground used for good or mundane purposes.

Without their trappings, opponents will not be able to nurture their idea and it will grow weaker and shrivel. The Servant must turn this to his advantage by seeing that these men continue to control their idea (but not their organizations), for should it fall into the hands of new men, they might revive the rival idea. So the Servant must preserve the original men in control of their idea (thus stifling their idea) for as long as possible. Although these men are beneath the notice of the Prince, and he would tend to neglect them totally, they must be brought to his notice by the Servant, entertained and, as proprietors of their idea, given honour by the Prince. The prestige invested in them will help them survive, and while they hold tight to their withering idea, it is very difficult for young men to prosper with a new idea. The Servant must never leave a vacuum in the world of ideas.

The Servant must understand that a man with nothing to lose is the most dangerous enemy, for he has time and colossal energy. However grand or small this man may be, he is still of very great danger. The Servant must remember that whenever a man is cast down totally, he bears a grudge. The Servant must also remember that the relatives of men who are frustrated in their aims, or cast down, often bear grudges as well. The Servant must prevent him or his relatives from causing trouble by making sure that this man is left with some position that he fears to lose. The role has to be carefully chosen, for under no circumstances must it be a position from which he can recover.

The Servant never corners enemies, especially the smaller ones; he further takes great care that the final dismissal of these small enemies should be delayed (a period of travel, a post overseas). Then, should they go and work for a rival, the information they bear with them about their employment will be long outdated. They must also be given great honour in their going, for it is the situation that people perceive, rather than the reality. If their situation looks better than that of others, it will be difficult for them to get the support of others for their trouble-making.

Great care must be taken in these matters, for the whole system of the Prince, the Idea and the Servant could be brought down by leaving one small man without hope. The small actions are the ones that tend to influence great events – one man and one pistol have changed history. Never neglect details.

Machiavelli talks about the merits of arming the population.

In some states citizen have been allowed to carry arms, while in others with conflicting philosophies they have not. There is no rule on this matter, for the ideas of each of these states have in time grown weak. The populations are no longer totally able to believe in them. So should citizens be armed or not? In fact, if they need arms, they will get them. But the Prince must see that his Idea is strong, for while it is, the population will not revolt and there will be no civil war. Only when the Idea becomes cluttered and deteriorates, so that it is merely a vehicle misused by lesser men, will they resort to arms. It is the strength of the Idea that is important to maintain the internal security of a nation. A strong nation will be well able to maintain its external security as suits the age in which it flourishes.

Although the Servant may plan with great care and proceed thoughtfully, one of the many elements which can destroy the best plans is the intelligent subordinate who, having been given an instruction, believes it to be foolish and changes it. Of course it is necessary for the Prince to employ subordinates of intelligence, for to be served by idiots would lead to downfall, and there is little point in telling the subordinate only to carry out instructions. This will inevitably cause antagonism in the subordinate and cause him either to work against the Servant or to leave.

However, it is beyond the capacity of the intelligent subordinate merely to carry out instructions without having his own thoughts about them. The Servant does not want to have to explain his plans, for this will lead to a series of debates and take too long. The Servant has to exercise much patience in the work he does, and none of it ought to be wasted on explanations. Even if the Servant has explained the plan and debated it with an intelligent subordinate, he is still likely to change the plan, making it a worse disaster than he already thinks it is. What does the Servant do? The Servant studies these intelligent subordinates, and considers how they may react to the Servant's plan, and he takes this into account. He will plan and counter-plan, so that if the first plan, being driven off course, founders, there will be another to put in its place.

How does the Servant treat the intelligent subordinate who has done this? The Servant explains his mistake, apologizing for the error of not informing the intelligent subordinate, claiming to have forgotten, and then congratulates him. Thus the Servant will have rebuked the intelligent subordinate, while also having displayed that human weakness which some confuse with humanity. The intelligent subordinate will tell all, helping the myth of the Servant, and enhancing the reputation of the Servant. In time, perhaps, the subordinate may become intelligent enough to obey without question.

It is one of the contradictions of his myth that the Servant, as well as seeming lazy and amiable, will have the reputation for hard work. This is acquired by letting people know the hours he works, for men are much impressed by long hours. They respond to time, not effort. But the Servant must never claim to be too busy, for if he were to do so, people will suggest to the Prince that he needs someone to help him. They would like the Servant always to be under observation, and as the Servant must do many things secretly, he needs nobody to help him. Nor must he have anyone of equal status in his office, only subordinates. To superiors, the Servant is as important or as humble as the occasion demands. The Servant must never allow himself to be allocated a position which defines his status.

The Servant must always give credit to another for his ideas. Firstly, he needs to encourage men to tell him their thoughts, so that he can use them in the service of the Prince. If he is known to steal their talent, they will be reluctant to do this. Secondly, there is nothing that provokes a man to anger so surely as to see another profit from the theft of his own ideas, and the anger of these men is not good for the Prince or for the Servant. Because they have talent, they could endanger the idea. Credit for men of talent must always be great. It will show the Servant's generosity of spirit, an important element in his myth.

The Servant must never try to do everything himself. He must always employ specialists to whom he will give credit for their work. Although, if their work is faulty, it is the Servant who must take the blame, for it is he who chose them.

A Servant must never expect more from people than they are capable of giving. It is important to remember this in the promotion of subordinates, for the Servant will be as strong as the ability of the people who work for him. Therefore, if he has a subordinate who is working well, it is rash to promote him. By doing so the Servant takes two risks. One is that the subordinate may not be as competent in the new job. The other is that the new replacement hired to carry out his former function may fail.

But while some men are content to perform the same task for great lengths of time, the best of them wish to be promoted. How can the Servant deal with this? First, he must, at the right moment, increase the wages of the subordinate, then – again at the right moment – change the title of his job without ever changing his function. Slowly, more responsibility must be given to the subordinate so that he always lives in hope. But the Servant avoids the trap of the sudden promotion, for it tends to lead to arrogance, and dismissal. The Servant must always praise his subordinates, showing kindness in their personal problems, but when they fail, the Servant must be ruthless and they must be made to vanish, to disappear into obscurity, yet feeling only great goodwill towards the Servant.

The Servant must study manners, and by this I do not mean the social graces. The Servant will need to suit his manner to all occasions, and his language too, for it is essential that he is understood; conversations often result in confusion, and the Servant should never assume that he has been understood.

It is possible to tell how a man will act from the manner of his speech. The Servant should learn this, for the manner in which a man orders his words will change as his thoughts change. The Servant will be able to detect the change before the individual concerned knows himself that he is about to change. These changes in men are so important they they cannot be too carefully watched, for it is these changes that unbalance events and bring danger to the Prince. As I have said before, a man whose whole approach to life is about to change will often exhibit this physically; there are telltale signs the Servant must watch for.

To mark a memorable occasion the Prince may desire to offer the Servant a gift and, wishing to be sure that he will enjoy this gift, may enquire what he would like. The choice is important. The value of the gift is no criterion. The only consideration is what gift the Servant should choose so that his choice will raise his standing in the Prince's eyes. He must not be accused of false modesty with a cheap gift, or of greed with an expensive one, of gluttony with food, of drunkenness with wine, of arrogance and ambition with estates, or with the hand of a woman who might create jealousy. No good will come of honours of this kind. The Servant must decide for himself. I only warn him of the danger.

Perhaps the best solution is to ask for something from the hand of the Prince, a speech inscribed, or a piece of philosophy written in the Prince's own hand. This gift combines flattery with economy. But, in future years, this memento could become of great value to the heirs of the Servant. Its worth in the auction rooms of another generation is, of course, dependent on the fame of the Prince, and may prove an additional spur to the Servant's desire for the Prince's success.

The Servant must be careful of very dull people for, although they lack the ingenuity to cause trouble for the Prince, there are many dull jobs to be done, and many dull people to do them. Together they amount to a vast force. They move slowly, they do not plot and plan, they are predictable – and herein lies the first danger. The Servant deals in the unpredictable, in change and in new situations. Dull people, on the other hand, change very slowly, and it is hard to tell when they actually have changed. Moreover, when they do so, because there are many of them, if they begin to reject the Servant and the Prince and the Idea, they can bring down any one of them. They may not know why they reject the Prince and the Idea, they may not even dislike him and his Idea, but politics is about collections of ill-informed opinions moving in one particular direction. It is about misinformation and half-formed judgements produced with certainty; these form waves of opinion that roll towards the beach. The Prince must ride these waves: indeed, his Idea must be the wave he rides. His Idea must become one of these waves but he must remember there is always a wave ahead of him and a wave behind him; he must join these waves with his wave, or the dull people, only half-thinking, will bring him down, for it has always been the tradition of dull people to offer as a sacrifice, their Prince.

There are no devices for controlling dull people. They can be motivated only occasionally by material benefits, more often by a curious sense of right and wrong. These two factors spring from the Idea: if it works, they will benefit materially. When the nation is wealthy these dull people will be calm, but there will be times when it is hard for the nation to achieve wealth. Then only the strongest ideas will survive. While it is taking root, they must feel that the Idea is right, and it is the use of the word 'right' which counts. Although they do not understand the Idea, they will follow what they believe is right. Do not imagine that the minds of dull people can be moved only by money.

Now the opponents of the Idea will try early on to disrupt its course in the hope of destroying it, and they will tell these dull people many reasons why they, too, should oppose it. The dull people will not believe them as long as they believe the Idea to be right. What the Prince and the Servant must do is promote the rightness of the Prince's Idea and make certain that material benefits flow from it before too long. Dull people have brought down rulers often before, and they are conscious of the great power which they can use to support or destroy the Prince; but being dull, they hesitate to use this great power.

As often as not what we call luck is something else, like inattention to detail by an opponent. The Servant eliminates luck as far as possible. He must plan to do without it and see that luck or acts of God do not affect the Idea. Essentially luck is good planning, although there is no point in planning for every eventuality. If it is going to rain, it will rain. Plan to avoid areas where rain matters.

Never neglecting details, the Servant must avoid an obsession with them as he plans. Other men have often said about attention to detail: 'Look after the pennies and the pounds will look after themselves.' It is more true to say: 'Look after the pennies and the pounds will go astray.' It is the overall concept that really matters: if the Idea is strong enough, it can overcome defects of detail. The Servant must never spend too much time on the detail of a strategy. He must plan on the grand scale, constructing his plan on experiences gained from knowledge of how men think and react. The Servant, the Prince, the Idea are nothing if they are not grand.

Having planned the Prince's luck, it must be put to good use. How the Servant chooses this use will be a matter of judgement, and it is by this judgement he will succeed or fail. Should he find that he is having a run of luck, he will begin to worry.

Planned luck is the study of the minutiae of events, something people seldom do. Apparently trivial events have gone by unnoticed and historians – having no explanation for them, or through slackness or the inability to identify what becomes lost with time – call them collectively luck. The Servant must not waste time studying all these minutiae. The practical advice to the Servant is to be well informed, to understand the habits of men, and to assemble a mass of different information; only then may he succeed in eliminating luck.

Machiavelli says: 'I conclude, therefore, that as fortune is changeable whereas men are obstinate in their ways, men prosper so long as fortune and policy are in accord, and when there is a clash they fail. I hold strongly to this: that it is better to be impetuous than circumspect; because fortune is a woman and if she is to be submissive it is necessary to beat and coerce her. Experience shows that she is more often subdued by men who do this than by those who act coldly. Always, being a woman, she favours young men, because they are less circumspect and more ardent, and because they command her with greater audacity.'

This is bad advice for the Prince and the Servant (and certainly as a method of dealing with women). It is evidence of the romantic fatalism that the Servant must avoid at all times, but it does catch the spirit of the Servant's myth and it is how he should appear in public. Fortune will play a large part in events, because it is beyond the capacity of men to control them. The Servant will study all the patterns of the lives and events that surround him and slowly place these patterns together. He acquires what romantic men call instinct. Although his actions are based on experience, he acts with the style of the romantic.

Machiavelli asserts that success follows those who are in accord with the spirit of the times. The Prince does not need to be in accord with the spirit of the times. He is the spirit of the times. By inspiring the Idea, the Prince will change fashion and that will become the expression of the spirit of the times.

Machiavelli, wondering how a Prince can rule well for a number of years and then fail, offers a number of causes. One he does not mention is the death wish in politics. Curiously, the Prince will be more likely to be subject to this death wish than lesser leaders. Although the tension involved in being a ruler is great, the tension of being *the* Prince is colossal. There may come times when the Prince will plot against himself as a means of deserting the Idea. Rulers will commonly train successors as a means of showing that they are not indispensable, and then dispense with them. This is not a sensible course of action, because it is a certain way of making enemies and because it gives credibility to these men which perhaps they do not deserve, having yet to prove themselves.

If the Idea is strong enough, it will survive the departure of a Prince, but only if it is handed to those who truly deserve it. A man who pretends to believe in the Idea but would use it only to gain power and then throw it on one side will gain nothing that is worth having. Such a man lives always with the necessity of pleasing this one or that one – he is a name in history, one on a list of names, but a figure of little consequence, famous perhaps only for how long he has ruled, not for how he held office. Not a Prince, not even a person, only a man of commerce without an idea.

The Servant must help the Prince to bear the burden of his situation, the claustrophobia and the inevitability of his continued rule. In these circumstances, the Servant must see that the Prince never actually appoints a successor, and if he does, the Servant appreciates that he must be dispensed with in a way that causes no trouble. When the Prince entertains a death wish, the Servant must provide diversions. The greater the Idea, the more difficult to carry out, the harder it is to bear. There is an argument that life is short and that therefore events should be lived for the day. For the Prince and his Servant, life is very long. Events move very slowly, and each day must be treated as if it were a lifetime. It is this extended time that will set off the death wish in the Prince. Being intelligent, he will suffer from the fear of never-ending life. There is no cure for this other than to direct the Prince's energies towards strengthening the Idea. In adversity, the competent seek to expand, the incompetent try to cut back. The Prince must extend the scope of his Idea when times are hard. He has no alternative, for if he is to reduce his Idea, this will weaken it, and if the Idea is weakened all will be lost. Many will try to persuade the Prince to trim his Idea. They must never be allowed to succeed.

The Prince will come under pressure through the fear of his supporters. When the Prince has ruled for a long time, his supporters will doubt his ability to retain power and the Prince, hearing their words, will doubt his own ability. Being tired and facing these doubters, many of whom he himself has placed in their positions, he will feel lonely. This loneliness is the danger for the Prince, for it is a kind of pain felt only by successful Princes, and only after many years.

Those who will doubt the Prince's ability to retain power most are those who claim to be his strongest supporters. His enemies respect the Prince's ability to retain power, for they have tried and failed to displace him. A successful Prince can only be displaced by his own, for only they can believe that they do the Prince a favour. The Prince, knowing them to be his friends and feeling the pain of loneliness, may let them have their way. The Servant believes them to be traitors. How can this situation be avoided? The Servant can do very little except try to see that the Prince never suffers from loneliness.

A most dangerous breed are the men who think they want power, know how to obtain it, and, when it is theirs, give it away. This trait many people might believe to be uncommon. The reverse, however, is true in the circles where the Servant moves, and it leaves the Prince in grave danger if a man like this is working closely with the Prince. This trait is another variety of the death wish. It has been said that these men are lazy, keener on the chase than the kill. It is possible that they need to acquire the power simply for the intellectual satisfaction it gives – for the personal pride rather than the public pride. All they need to know is that power can be theirs; then they give it away. This is one of life's greatest conceits. It shows a kind of mental arrogance and, perhaps, a fear of not being able to hold on to power and of having it taken away. Although they do not seem to mind the mental humiliation of giving power away, this is in fact a form of controlled masochism. These men are very unreliable and the Servant must be alert to the first signs of this phenomenon. This is not failure, for these men do as they wish.

Machiavelli talks of failure, which is not a subject that absorbs us because this is not a handbook for the inadequate, but an argument that the Prince fully in possession of his Idea will succeed. This book has attempted to show how the Servant can help in this aim. Machiavelli talks of Princes reigning by the use of skill. Here we are talking about a Prince reigning through the strength of the Idea. The Servant's skill makes this possible, but the Idea will transcend the rule of Princes and the practice of Servants, until at last it is weakened by being diluted with the thoughts of others. It becomes cluttered by the parafanatics, and weakened further by their laziness. After the Prince and the Servant have gone, then only the very strongest Idea will survive, and only if it is taken up by another who may become a Prince. Thus the Prince must, in time, give thought to an heir.

There will come a time in the life of all Servants when the Prince has held power for many years and when the Idea of the Prince will be passing through a period of disrepute. Rivals will be gathering their strength to challenge the Prince. Many of the Prince's erstwhile supporters will have left the Prince's councils and some secretly and some publicly will harbour resentment towards him. Many of the Prince's current supporters will wonder how much longer the Prince can last. The Prince's enemies will attack the Prince's Idea, and his supporters will have doubts and wonder whether the Idea should be made more palatable to the people. This changing of the Idea is unacceptable to the Prince and to the Servant, for the Idea cannot be changed for political convenience. The current supporters of the Prince are worried about this, for they believe that the Prince has only a past and that they must secure their future. The leaders to whom these men might be drawn are men of convenience, none of them having a real Idea, none of them having a real body of support.

So the Prince believes that he is secure and, indeed, he is secure, for the majority of these groups support the Prince in preference to any one of the others who would be rulers. But fellow travellers of the Prince who call themselves supporters talk among themselves and do not always report the truth of their discussions. Out of these discussions will come rumours that the Prince is going to be overthrown by one of the rivals of the fellow travellers. And so his source of security, the split loyalties of the past, becomes the Prince's very danger. These fellow travellers will combine against one of their number who seems likely to defeat the Prince, and seek a new champion. In the end the Prince will have to throw the weight of his small band of loyal supporters behind one of the contestants who seems to support the Idea. His only option is to overcome those who had previously tried to overcome him, and so preserve the hope of a future for his Idea.

There will be confusion and plotting among men who pledge their loyalty lightly, and self-interest will prevail. The Prince will be defeated and the new leader will proclaim the Idea, adjusted for convenience; but he does not have the Idea, nor is he, without the Idea, the Prince. It is the role of the Servant to prevent these events. When these events happen it is the beginning of the end for the Idea, and when the Idea begins to weaken it is finished, and no use at all to the people.

The true Servant must never offer to resign. The Prince cannot possibly accept his resignation. The Servant must not test his relationship with the Prince, for a Prince with whom he might do so is not worth the title. The Servant, if he believes the circumstances important, must organize his dismissal. Only he can judge if and when the Prince could be better served. Neither the courtiers, nor the people, nor even the Prince can judge the moment.

In times of extreme trouble, the populace and the Prince's supporters may look for a sacrifice. By tradition, the sacrifice is the Prince himself, but since the Prince must survive, the Servant will give the crowd a substitute: he must sacrifice himself. But the crowd is unlikely to be satisfied with a Servant, so he must arrange that the Prince clothe him in honour and speak of him as a Prince. The Servant must wear the robes of a Prince, look like a Prince and, for the first time, behave like one. Only then should he be sacrificed. And then only, the Servant can cast himself into the hands of the crowd. He must not ask the Prince to carry out this deed. It must be carried out properly in every respect. No hesitation, no half measures, for saving the Prince to carry on the Idea is the ultimate purpose of the Servant. It is an end that gives him true nobility.

In contemplating this act, the Servant must ask himself whether he has an alternative. Has he taken all known human emotions into account? Is he still sure that there is no choice? Has he taken into account the possibility of the unexpected? Only when he has thought about these matters thoroughly can he make this decision. Sacrificing the Servant will come as a complete surprise to the enemies of the Prince. They cannot expect this, for it was neither in the Prince's character, nor in his mind. It is the idea and action of the Servant. The only independent action that the Servant ever takes.

[ 95 ]

The surprise (the more so because the Prince, having heaped rewards on the Servant, will have increased dislike of him by both enemy and friend, thus making his sacrifice more effective) will give a great advantage to this Prince, allowing him to make a tactical retreat, regroup his Idea, engage a new Servant, and transform this unexpected turn of events into a lasting victory.

The Servant requires courage, loyalty and passion. He should always adopt the heroic position, for in defeat he will find the greatest victory.

# EPILOGUE

Eventually there is a time for change, and when it comes, it will sweep far and wide. All our boundaries have changed, all the values that we believed true in the past seem worthless. Sent into the wilderness, the Prince will be reviled. But let the Servant take heart. Let him watch every moment of this change, for in time it will come again and his heroes will become the icons of the future. His Prince will again become the Prince, and his Idea will be restored.

The Servant must consider carefully how to conduct the affairs of the Prince in this empty time. He must consider whether he truly believes in the Idea and the Prince. If not, he should leave politics and take up agriculture. If he believes, the Servant must stay and serve the Prince and the Idea. No other Prince, however attractive, or, for that matter, however successful, is of any use to the Servant. The Servant must wait and arrange the affairs of the Prince, always keeping the Prince and the Idea pure and in readiness, for who can tell how the affairs of men may change again? The Servant must remember that the memories of men are very short and, after an interval, a useful Servant can recall the events that suit the Prince, and the population will remember them with joy, forgetting all else. These memories can form the base for the return of the Prince and his Idea. In fact, of course,

Princes seldom return. More often, they return as the patrons of their Idea, using their Idea to shape events during their lives and readying their Idea to live long after them.

## ACKNOWLEDGEMENTS

I would like to thank Stephen Fay for all his help
and encouragement.

Quotations from Machiavelli's *The Prince*
are taken from the Penguin edition,
translated by George Bull (1961).